The Devil Wears Timbs III

Tranay Adams

The Devil Wears Timbs III

Hell On Earth

A Novel by *Tranay Adams*

Tranay Adams

First Edition January 2015
Printed in the United States of America

This is a work of fiction. Names, characters, places, and incidents either are products of the author's imagination or are used fictitiously. Any similarity to actual events or locales or persons, living or dead, is entirely coincidental.
Email: trnayadams@gmail.com
Facebook: Tranay Adams
Cover design and layout by: Sunny Giovanni
Book interior design by: Shawn Walker
Edited by: Shawn Walker

Acknowledgments

If I told you how many times that I nodded off at my laptop writing this trilogy I'm certain that you wouldn't believe me. Every time my head would hit the keys I'd snap right awake and get back to completing these stories. At times my chest would be aching like a mothafucka and I could feel my heart raging inside of my chest. I could hear my conscience saying, 'Say, bruh, it's time for your ass to go to sleep. We're tired than a mothafucka. We can finish this shit tomorrow.' I would entertain the idea, but then I think of those who hit me up. 'Tranay, when is The Devil Wears Timbs II, or III coming out'? Tranay, I love your writing style and how you tell a story. Tranay, you're my new favorite author. Tranay, your story touched me. I had to take care of my brother because my mother was on drugs like Eureka's mom. Tranay, you're Young CA$H (Priscilla Murray, I'm flattered, that's man's a beast with that pen).

My supporters are the best that there is and you drive me to be better than I was yesterday. It is amazing to me how people that you've never laid eyes on can make you feel that you're so special. Your words make my heart skip a beat and I feel the butterflies in my stomach. Goddamn, I done fell in love with y'all, man. Got me out here simping and shit lol Nah, I'm kidding. I cannot thank you all enough, when I say that I LOVE YOU I'm so sincere. I mean it with all that I am. If you were here right now I would hug you and tell you to your face. Thank you for coming on this literary journey with me. I hope you stay on this ride and never want to get off. Shawn Walker, my editor, you're the best. This is a marriage. You can forget about a divorce. This shit is for life.

Hookah, I know you didn't think I was going to forget about you? How could I? You would never let me hear the end of it. I am happy to have you on my short list of people that I call 'FRIEND'. You're beautiful. You're outside matches your insides.
Click! Clack!
Carlito's Voice: Okayyyyy, I'm reloaded!!!

CHAPTER ONE

"Are you alright?" Eureka inquired.

"She—she took—she took my safe." Fear uttered, still harboring a faraway look. "That was all of the money that I had in the world!" his eyes became glassy and his top lip twitched as he gritted his teeth. "It's all—it's all *fucking gone!*"

"Fear?" She slowly approached him, taking cautious steps in his direction.

Hearing her voice snapped his attention in her direction. He was coherent now. He pointed his banger at her and her hands shot up in the air. Her heart quickened. She was scared.

Fear's eyes glinted with madness. He was gritting his teeth so hard his top lip trembled. "Y'all set me up!" He grumbled, motioning the gun between her and Anton.

"Fuck are you talking about?" Anton asked.

"We didn't set chu up!" Eureka frowned. "Fear, I swear to God we didn't know that this was going to happen. You gotta believe us."

"Fuck y'all! Both of y'all!" Fear shouted. His eyebrows arched and his nose wrinkled. "I ain't gotta believe shit. You die now!"

"Baby, we didn't set chu up," Eureka spoke sincerely. "Think about it. Wouldn't it have been better for us to leave you laid face down back up in the mountains, then shoot back here to get the safe so that we wouldn't have to worry about a situation like this?"

The killer held his gun on the siblings as he milled it over inside of his head. After rationalizing what she'd said, he let the hand holding his gun fall to his side. He stepped backwards and plopped down on the steps. He rested his banger in his lap and ran a hand down his face, trying to calm himself. Eureka sat down beside him. She wrapped her arms around him and placed his head against her chest. He closed his eyes and tried to wrap his head around what the hell just happened to him.

Fear shook his head. "What am I gonna do?"

Eureka lay her head against his shoulder and hooked her arm around his, caressing his hand with hers. "What the fuck am I gonna do?" He thought about the life savings Giselle had taken him for. He had every dollar to his name inside of that safe and now it was gone. If Eureka and Anton's mother ever resurfaced, he knew without a doubt he would body her ass.

"I don't know, baby, but we'll figure something out." Eureka tried to console him.

"Fuckkkkk!" he screamed, slamming his palm up against his forehead. He bit down on his curled finger and then laid his hand on his knee, exhaling. "Alright, I need to get to the hospital to get this wound patched up, before it gets   infected."

"Okay, let me lock the house up." Eureka told him, before ducking off inside.

Fear rose to his feet and tucked his gun on his hip just as Anton was approaching.

"Yo, man, I'm sorry about all of this." He looked up at the killer with sorrowful eyes.

Looking down at his protégé, Fear couldn't help but feel sorry for him. He couldn't image what it was like to be in his shoes, go through what he had, and have a mother like Giselle. It wasn't his fault that his old lady was a dope fiend and as scandalous as they come. The kid didn't have a choice but to play the hand that he was dealt.

Fear exhaled and threw his arm around the little nigga's shoulders and pulled him close, walking him toward the car.

"Don't worry about it, G." He told him. "Sometimes shit happens and there isn't anything that you can do about it."

Although the killer was acting cool and calm on the outside, on the inside he was boiling hot. Wherever Giselle had gone, she'd better stay there because if he should ever see her face again he was going to blow it off.

*****

Ding!

The elevator chimed before its double doors slid apart and a group of men filed out. Ronny wore a mask of determination as he moved down the corridor with Vladimir by his side and his men bringing up the rear. Every man accounted for held a shotgun, handgun, or assault rifle of his own. They walked around with their weapons out in the open as if that shit wasn't illegal. Stopping at a green door with #9 on it, Vladimir hoisted up his M-16 and wrapped its strap around his fist. He then turned to Ronny, looking him over before eventually speaking. "Is this the right place?" he asked.

"Yeah, this is the right place." Ronny frowned and gritted his teeth, causing the veins in his neck to bulge. They looked like they were about to explode. Malvo had violated and now his ass had to pay. "Step aside," He kicked the door at the lock. *Boom! Boom!*

The door snapped open sending a splinter of wood and the loose bronze chain across the room. Ronny,

Vladmir and the Russian spilled in on high alert, swaying their weapons and ready to leave a nigga a memory.

"Move in and stop the pulse of anything moving!" the Russian drug lord ordered. With his M-16 pointed and ready, his armed men approached he and Ronny's rear. They moved inside of the living room and two shabbily dressed dope fiends dropped the fifty inch flat-screen they were carrying. The TV hit the floor and fell on its tinted black screen, cracking it as a couple of sparks flew.

"Who are you?" Vladimir barked with a scrunched face. "Where the fuck is Malvo?"

The dope fiends held their trembling hands up in the air, their heads snapped around at all of the angry faces with their weapons pointed at them. Their legs began to shake and they could feel their dicks growing hot as piss filled their bladders.

"Wh—what?" One of the fiend's stammered.

"Nigga, you betta start saying a lot more than *what* if you don't wont cho melon blown off yo shoulders!" Ronny spat, with spit jumping off of his lips. The skin of his forehead pulled tight at his eyebrows and his nostrils pulsated.

"We're—we're just a couple dope heads, man." The fiend told him. "No one's been in this place for months, so we broke in here to see if we could lift the TV for a couple of dollas, is all!" He swallowed hard and prayed he didn't feel the onslaught of hot pellets.

"Arggggh!" The other fiend doubled over to vomit from lack of heroin. The sudden movement startled Ronny and he snapped his shotgun to him, pulling the trigger. *Bloom!* The impact sent the fiend through the window, shattering the glass and hurling down to the crowded streets below. A soft thud, the swerving of cars and their horns could be heard from the apartment.

"Oh, God, please." The surviving fiend's legs shook wildly as he dropped to his knees. He trembled and clasped his hands together, begging. He was scared as shit. He didn't want to end up a blood stain on the carpet for the crime lab to examine. Tears threatened to seep from the corners of his eyes and his bottom lip quaked. A dark spot expanded at his crotch and he whizzed down his leg, soiling   the   floor.

Seeing that Ronny had the situation under control, Vladimir lowered his M-16 at his side and approached the window. He took a quick look down at the streets and saw people abandoning their cars to check on the sprawled dead body. He then turned to Ronny, watching how he handled his business.

"Please, man, please..." The fiend groveled, hoping that he'd be spared.

Ronny lifted his shotgun and pressed it at the center of the junky's forehead, allowing his finger to rest on the trigger. Sweat rolled down the man's forehead as he closed his eyes and swallowed. He said a prayer to God as he waited to be cast out into The Land of the Dead.

The thought of wetting the fiend up, went back and forth across Ronny's mind like a ping pong ball. He could easily burst his melon but it wouldn't do anything for him. His life wasn't the one he wanted to take. It was Malvo's. And he wanted it badder than a virgin wanted his first piece of pussy. Ronny exhaled and lowered his weapon to his side, looking down at his prey with pity. The junky's eyes slowly peeled open one at a time and looked around before settling on the man standing before him.

"Get outta here." Ronny threw his head toward the door.

The dope fiend grabbed him by the leg of his jeans. "Thank you, man! Thank you, young brotha! God bless you!"

"Get the fuck out here before I change my mind," Ronny stated sternly.

"You got it. I'm outta here." He got up on his feet and hurried for the door.

Ronny turned around to him as he went, "And keep your mouth shut! I don't wanna have to come looking for you!"

"You ain't gotta worry about me, I'm not gone."

Rattt!

The fiend's face went flying across the living room when the assault rifle's copper-bullet entered through the back of his skull. He fell face down into the carpet with the heels of his tattered sneakers coming up and then falling back down onto the floor. His arms came plopping down onto the carpet along with what was left of his head.

Ronny looked from the dead body to over his shoulder where the bullet was fired from. He found Vladimir with his M-16's stock braced against his shoulder as he gripped it firmly with an eye lined up with the sighting. The Russian lowered the rifle and allowed it to dangle at his side.

"No witnesses," he said, before motioning for his henchmen to follow him as he treaded out of the apartment.

*****

"Hey, baby?" Malvo spoke into the phone.

"What's up, boo?" An older gentleman's voice responded.

The lines on Malvo's forehead deepened. "Who the fuck is this?"

"Take a wild guess."

Malvo's eyes snapped open and he sat up on the couch. "Siska?"

"What did I tell you, Malvo? What did I tell you, huh?"

"Daddyyyy!" Heaven's voice rang out in the background.

"Malvoooo!" Faith's voice rang out after her daughter's.

Hearing his family in distress caused his heart to skip a beat.

"Look, man, I got the money, I can…"

"No! Fuck the money, you pay now with their lives."

"No! Wait, I…"

Boc! Boc!

Shots echoed from the other end of the telephone and the call disconnected. Malvo dropped to his hands and knees onto the floor, choked up by what he'd just heard. He stared ahead at nothing making a weird groaning sound. His eyes welled up with tears and ran down his face. He felt like someone had torn his beating heart out of his chest. He couldn't fathom the pain he was experiencing because he'd never felt it before. But the people he had victimized throughout his selfish existence of a life had and now it was his turn.

Boom! Boom! Boom!

His front door rattled and his neck snapped in its direction. Something told him that it was Karma that had come to pay him a visit and he grabbed his banger off of the coffee table. He rose to his feet and pointed the gun at the door. If it was death coming to claim him on the other side of that door, he wasn't going out without a fight.

"You wanna bang, cock sucka?" he barked, spittle flying from his lips and tears sliding down his face. "Well, let's bang!"

"Malvo! Malvo!" A voice rang from the opposite side of the door. "It's Crunch, man! Let me in!"

Malvo closed his eyes and exhaled with a sigh of relief. He slowly lowered his tool and wiped his forehead with the back of his chunky hand. He listened to the pounding on the door for a time longer before starting for it, wiping the tears from his cheeks as best as he could. He removed the chain and unlocked the door, pulling it open.

Crunch stood where he was frozen in shock once he laid eyes on his boss. Creases appeared on his forehead. He could tell by his glassy looking eyes and damp face that he had been crying. Malvo stepped aside and he made his way inside, heading for the living room. Malvo followed right behind him, pouring himself a drink once he reached the bar   area.

"What's the emergency?" Malvo asked, sitting the bottle down and taking the glass to the head. The dark skinned hoodlum watched as his mans drank the brown liquor as if it was water.

"Yo, fam, everything alright?" Crunch asked concerned.

Holding the glass at his mouth, the dope dealer licked his lips. "Everything is copasetic." He drank the hard liquor down.

"What's the news that'll blow my fuse?"

He placed his hand on his shoulder and looked into his eyes. "Siska." He closed his eyes tightly and shook his head, fighting back the tears that were dying to be released. He sucked his lips inward and took a deep breath. He peeled his eyelids open. "Siska, killed Faith and Heaven."

Crunch's jaw dropped when he received the news. He was devastated. He walked away from Malvo with his hands clutching both sides of his head, pacing the floor. "Jesus Christ." He stopped where he was and walked back over to the big man. "Damn, I'm sorry, man. I'm so fucking   sorry."

"I'm fucked up, C. I'm real fucked up behind this." Malvo confessed in his moment of vulnerability. He'd never been the type of nigga to talk about his feelings. He dealt with them the best way he knew how and that was handlings them internally. "This shit done took me to a dark place, a very dark place. I'm not gon' ever be right after this." He poured up another glass. "I gotta go out there though, man. I gotta go out there to see for myself that they're really gone. And I want chu to drive me."

Crunch's hands were on his hips as he listened to Malvo talk. He was staring at the floor but he looked up, nodding his head.

"Alright, I'll take you." He agreed. He ran a hand down his face. "Look, I hate to be the bearer of bad news, but Ronny's back."

Malvo frowned when he heard this. He sat the blunt down in the ashtray that he'd just fired up and approached Crunch.

"He was at Antoinette's house?" he asked, planting both of his hands on his shoulders.

"Yep and guess who he was with?" Malvo's forehead contracted as he waited out the dramatic pause for his answer. "Vladimir and the rest of those Russian niggaz."

"Shit! Shit! Shit!"

"What? What's wrong?"

"We've gotta get outta here." Malvo said. "Ronny knows all of my spots. They're going to hit us."

"Why on earth would the Russians be looking to hit chu?"

This froze Malvo because he didn't know what he could say that wouldn't deter Crunch.

"Think about it." He turned around to Crunch. "Who knows what he told Vladimir to get him and his people to go along with coming after me?"

"Right." Crunch nodded, rubbing the back of his neck.

Five minutes later the men vanished from the apartment. The only indication that someone had been there was a glass of liquor and a burning blunt.

*****

The shadows began to stir as someone was moving within them. A moment later a hooded person stepped before Giselle, blowing a cloud of smoke and dumping ashes on the floor. She tried to peer closely to see who it was standing before her but her efforts were useless. The shade that the hood provided coupled with the darkened room hid the person's face.

"Who—who are you?" Giselle asked timidly as her heart thumped inside of her chest. It was so hot that sweat rolled down her face and obscured the vision in her right eye. Taking the sleeve of her jacket, she wiped her eye and face.

Constance stopped in front of Giselle and then she was able to make out the face through the bluish light shone through the gated window. She licked her lips and smiled   evilly.

"I am the devil." She spread her arms apart and looked about the room. "And this is hell." Constance laughed hard and manically.

"Oh, shit! Helllllp! Helllllp me!" Giselle screamed as loudly as she could, yanking the chain her wrist was shackled to, trying to break free. "Helllllp! Oh, God, pleaseeee!   Somebody   helllllp   meeeeee!"

While Giselle screamed and yanked on the chain, Constance   continued   to   laugh   hysterically. "Hahahahahahahahaha!"

"Please!" Giselle screamed again, wondering why she was the one to be held prisoner by that fucking psychopath.

"Shut the fuck up, bitch. Ain't nobody gon' hear you down here."

Crack! Brack! Whack!

Constance's Timberland boot was like a blur as it swept across Giselle's temple, mouth and chin. Giselle fell flat on her back, pain etched upon her face as she looked around like she didn't know where she was. Her tongue moved around inside of the pit of blood that was her mouth. She slowly got upon her hands and knees, spitting blood as if she was vomiting. Long red slime hung from her lips as she spit onto the cold floor. With teary eyes she looked up at her kidnapper, wiping her mouth with her freehand.

"Why? Why are you doing this?" she asked.

Constance reached inside of her back pocket and pulled out something. She tossed it beside Giselle's hand. Lines formed on her forehead as she looked down, wondering where she'd gotten the old picture of her and her family. She picked it up, looking from it to the mad woman standing over her.

"Where did you get this from?"

"Your daughter," Constance spat. "The lil' home-wrecker weaseled her way into my house and snatched my man right from under me." She blew smoke from out of her nostrils and mouth then dropped the burning L at her feet, mashing it out under the heel of her boot. "She took something I loved, so I figured I'd take something that she loves.   You."

"Wait a minute, I…"

Wooof! Wooof! Woook!

Constance's legs twisted at funny angles in midair and she brought her boot across Giselle's jaw, dislodging a bloody tooth. The red tooth tumbled along the floor and settled in the crevasse of the drain. The last blow knocked Giselle out cold, leaving on her side snoring.

"That's right. Get plenty of rest 'cause I'm far from through with your ass." Constance studied her handiwork for a time before walking out of the boiler room.

Tranay Adams

CHAPTER TWO

Eureka sat in the lobby of Kaiser Hospital hunched over in a chair, fidgeting with her fingers. From the expression on her face you could tell she was in deep thought.

When she looked up, she found a little boy turned around in his chair facing her. His face was solemn and his innocent eyes studied her curiously. She reasoned he was wondering what was on her mind. So, Eureka mustered up a halfhearted smile which caused one to slowly form on the boy's face. The boy hesitantly waved at her and she waved back.

"Jaelyn Henderson." The receptionist called out from the door where she was looking over a clipboard.

"Come on, Jaelyn." The boy's mother took him by the hand, ushering him toward the door the receptionist was at. For some reason the little boy couldn't tear his eyes away from Eureka. In fact, his eyes didn't waiver until he disappeared through the door.

"Here you go." Anton approached from her left, carrying two Styrofoam cups of coffee. He passed one of them to his sister and sat down beside her. He was about to take a sip of the hot black liquid when he noticed the worriment on her face. "Watts up?"

Eureka shook her head shamefully. "Mommy, I can't believe the shit she pulled tonight."

"You're telling me?" Anton raised an eyebrow. "I got sixteen stitches in the back of my dome and almost caught an ass full of lead on the account of her. Fuck, mommy!" he spat harshly.

"I know you're hot right now, so I know you don't mean that."

"I don't?" He looked at her like *Are you sure about that?* "I'm sick and tired of mommy and her bullshit. We've been giving her a pass for how many years 'cause of her addiction? She's been using that shit as a crutch and we've been enabling her. Sometimes you just gotta sit back and look at cha life. I know she has. You can't tell me she hasn't. She just doesn't give a fuck about changing, about us."

"Anton..."

He shook his head and cut her off. "Uh uh, ain't nothing you can say to get me to look at things differently. I see life for what it is."

"What chu mean?" she frowned.

"Shit is all bad with very lil' good." He spoke his beliefs. "You either adjust or get gobbled up." She nodded her understanding. "I've developed this *I don't give a fuck* mentality. So if you ain't L.O.E yo' ass is food. I'll never be a victim again. From now on I'll make them."

Her brows furrowed and she took a closer look at him. "You've grown cold, baby brother."

"So you say, but I call it adjusting." His eyes shifted to a door that two patients were coming out of. One of them was Fear. He was carrying a white bag with RX on it and walking in their direction. "Here comes the H.N.I.C now." He tapped Eureka. Seeing her man, she stood up and ran over to him. They embraced and kissed. She then helped him over to a seat that was beside hers and Anton's.

"You alright?" Anton inquired.

"I'm straight, family," he answered. "They stapled me up, gave me some pain killers, and sent me on my way."

"What happens now?" Eureka asked, stroking his hand as it lay in her lap.

"Nothing has changed." He assured them. "We go after The West Coast Connection."

"Who do we hit first?" Anton asked excitedly, rubbing his hands together. He couldn't wait to push a couple of niggaz' scalps back.

"That's a no brainer," Eureka interjected. "Bemmy."

"Nah," Fear shook his head. "I want Niles to see his entire world collapsing around him so he'll know he's living on borrowed time, and right when he's cornered with his heart raging inside of his chest and piss threatening to seep out of his bladder that's when I'll introduce his ass to the Grim Reaper." He scowled and grinded his teeth as he clenched his fist. When he finally caught up to Niles, there was going to be hell to pay.

Fear thought back to the night at the restaurant when he'd had the meeting with The West Coast Connection. On his way out of the parking lot, he hopped out of his car and placed a tracking device underneath Bemmy's vehicle, so he'd always know where the OG was. That would make him easier to find when it came time to make him part ways with his life.

"Yeah," he stared straight ahead at nothing. "Ol' Niles will be the last to die."

*****

The whole ride out to Rancho Cucamonga, Malvo was chain smoking and impatiently tapping his foot on the floor, trying to prepare himself for the inevitable. Whatever he found once he made it to Faith's parents' house, he was sure he wouldn't be ready for it. He couldn't help himself though. He had to go through with it. Not only was curiosity getting the best of him, but he wouldn't be able to sleep a wink at night if he didn't check things out for himself.

Crunch double parked in the middle of the street outside of Faith's parents' crib. He and Malvo hopped out and pulled their guns. They speed walked toward the house, taking in everything around them. It was dark out and there wasn't a soul present. Looking upon the porch they noted that the front door was cracked open.

"All bad, all fucking bad," Crunch said under his breath, low enough for the big man not to hear him.

Malvo darted up the stairs with Crunch on his heels. He kicked open the front door and waved his banger around. He and his comrade moved about cautiously, careful not to make a sound like a couple of cops that had been called upon a scene. It wasn't until they reached the kitchen that they lowered their weapons.

The men stood side by side at the kitchen doorway looking everything over. There were smears of blood on the white tiled floor, refrigerator and cabinets, sticky with specs of brain matter. Crunch closed his eyes and shook his head. He could only imagine what his nigga was going through. He looked to him and gripped his shoulder in a form of comfort. Malvo blinked his eyes to help him see straight, moving his head as if he was reading something on a typewriter. His lips came apart and he staggered back, holding both sides of his head. He squeezed his eyes closed tightly. He could hear Siska, Faith and his daughter over and over again inside of his head, loud and clear.

"What did I tell you, Malvo? What did I tell you, huh?"

"Daddyyyy!"

"Malvoooo!"

"Look, man, I got the money. I can..."

"No. No! No! No! Fuck the money. You pay now with their lives."

"No! Wait, I..."

Boc! Boc!

"Noooooooooooo!" His eyes snapped open and he screamed at the top of his lungs, causing that thing at the back of his throat to shake. His eyes blurred as they filled with tears and streamed down his face. He dropped down to his hands and knees. "Oh, my God. Faith, I'm so sorryyyy!" His head nodded as his mouth widen. He hollered in emotional pain, but the sound didn't come into sync until later. He bowed his head to the carpet and clenched his hands into fists, screaming into the floor and muffling the sound.

Crunch wore a shocked expression with lines across his forehead watching his boss' tantrum. Having seen enough, he grabbed him by the front of his shirt and pulled him up, forcing him up against the wall. He stared into his face as he hollered out.

"Pull yourself together." Crunch shook him roughly as he clenched his teeth. "Get it together goddamn it!" Malvo continued to bawl. It was like he hadn't even said anything. He then cocked his ashy black hand back, smacking him back and forth across his face viciously. The assault snapped the big man out of his trance. He stared ahead trembling with glassy eyes and a red nose. Tight lipped, he sniffled like a four year old that had been spanked. "Are you with me, huh? Look at me, man." Malvo slowly turned his face to Crunch. He closed his eyes and swallowed, nodding his head.

Crunch heard faint police sirens heading for their location. He snatched the curtain open and peered outside. Neighbors were gradually emerging from their homes to see what was going on.

"We've gotta get the fuck up from outta here. The Boys are on the way and there's a bunch of nosey mothafuckaz outside." He told Malvo but he didn't receive a response. Malvo was staring off into space, occasionally blinking and talking gibberish. "Aye, aye, aye," he snapped his fingers before his eyes until he came to. "You hear me, nigga?"

"What?"

"The police are on the way."

"Oh, shit."

"*Oh shit*, is right. Let's go." He tapped his arm and ran out of the house with him following suit.

*****

Malvo rolled in the front passenger seat of his truck stuck in a trance. He couldn't believe how karma had come back to bite him in the ass. Damn near all of his life he'd been a pain in someone's ass, and now it was someone's turn to be one in his. He never thought about the possibility of his chickens coming home to roost. At least not like that.

He expected niggaz to come gunning for him, but his family? Not in a million years. Granted he didn't have any reserves on how he'd gotten at Ronny, but he never expected for Siska to get at him like he did. The old man was a throwback gangsta who followed a set of old school rules so for him to get at him like that was unorthodox.

The play the Greek laid down fucked his world up. All he wanted to do was ball up, cry and then die. But as bad as he wanted to, he couldn't do that because he didn't want to be remembered like that in the streets. When the curtains finally closed, he wanted niggaz to glorify his name and speak of how he'd given it up in the trenches. He wanted to be known as a legend like the generation of G's before him.

"Malvo! Malvo!"

Malvo snapped back to the here and now after he heard Crunch calling his name. He looked around as if he didn't know where he was. He took in the scenery and then realized he was riding shotgun with his capo behind the wheel. He settled back in the seat and rummaged around inside of his pocket as he listened to Crunch.

"We're gonna settle the score with this nigga, Siska, you hear me?"

Malvo sparked up a cigarette and tilted his head back, blowing cloud of smoke into the air. He then held down a button that let down the window, letting out the smoke.

"That's what we on now," Malvo said, somewhat back to his normal self. "The kid gloves are off. I'm getting it in with this prick. Ain't nobody gon' be spared. Mothers, kids, side bitches, aunts, uncles, nephews, even the fucking family dog. I don't give a fuck no more, Crunch. We're out here." He scratched his chin with the hand he held the square in and looked to him. "Mothafuckaz took my heart and my rib, so now they gotta feel my pain." His eyes were glassy and twinkled with insanity. He looked like a man with nothing to lose and ready to go all out with it.

Crunch nodded his understanding as he pushed the truck along. He reached over and touched fists with Malvo. The city wasn't prepared for the gangsta shit they were about to lay down.

*****

Vladimir's limousine pulled up outside of Ronny's house and he hopped out. He'd just stepped upon the curb when he was called back. He turned around and threw his head back like *what's up?*

"This is just the beginning, my friend," the Russian drug lord told him. "We're not gonna stop until this dick-head comes out of hiding. Be ready tomorrow, I'll send for you."

Ronny nodded and went on about his business. Heading toward his house, he gave himself the once over. There were splatters of blood on his sweat suit and his Timbs. He and the Russians spent most of their night kicking in the doors of Malvo's traps, laying down their pressure   game.

Four trap boys sat on their knees with their wrists bound behind their backs and duct-tape over their mouths. The Russians stood behind them with their M-16s pointed at the back of their heads. They weren't focused on them, though. Nah, Ronny had their undivided attention. He was standing before them beside a pile of money and dope. He drenched everything with gasoline and discarded the gas-can, slinging it aside. He struck a match across the lower half of the trap boy's face who wasn't wearing duct-tape over his mouth and a flame ignited.

"*Nigga, do you know whose shit this is?*" *The trap boy asked.*

Ronny pulled off his ski-mask and revealed his identity, the trap boy gasped. He couldn't believe his eyes.

"*I know exactly whose it is, and I'm leaving you alive so you can tell who was responsible for this carnage.*" *He dropped the match onto the pile. Froooosh! The flames engulfed it, starting their feast. Ronny gave the Russians a nod and they fired their assault rifles in a domino effect, dropping the trap boys on by one. The last trap boy had closed his eyes when the shots were fired and blood splattered against both sides of his face. When he looked from left to right he saw the dead bodies of his homies lying on both sides of him, with their brain and blood oozing out the back of their heads.*

The youngster closed his eyes and swallowed hard, looking shaken up after seeing his people get laid the fuck out. While that was happening, the Russians made homemade torches. They kicked over the sofa and love seat and set them on fire. From there they lit up the curtains and anything else that would ignite.

Ronny stared down at the young nigga who looked like he was about to fall apart at the seams. He exhaled and brought his open palm back and forth across his face viciously.

Smack! Smack! Smack!

"*Aye, aye, aye,*" *he called out until he got his attention.* "*Snap out of it. Are you with me?*" *He nodded yes as he began to tremble all over.* "*Good. When you finally get a hold of that fat muthafucka, you be sure to tell him that Ronny did this, alright? Ronny Montgomery, you hear   me?*"

"*Yea—yeah,*" *he nodded rapidly.*

"Let me hear you say it then."

"Ron—Ronny Montgomery did this." He stuttered.

"Good boy." He patted his cheek and signaled for Nicolay to open the door. He did just that and the trap boy stood to his feet. With his wrists still bound behind his back, he ran as fast as he could out of the door. Ronny watched him go before turning his attention to the raging fire. It was devouring everything within range.

"Ronny!" Mikhail called after him. When he looked, he was standing by the door along with the rest of the Russians. He threw his head toward the door like, Come on.

"I'm right behind you." He told them and they went on out of the house. He looked at his sweats and his boots and saw the blood splattered on them. He shrugged and folded his arms across his chest. He stood there watching the flames dance around the room eating whatever they came across. He closed his eyes, exhaled, and made his way out of the house.

Ronny opened the door of his house and stepped inside. It was dark save for the light over the stove. He closed the door behind him, hung his keys on one of the hooks of the key-holder, and sat down on the couch. He tilted his head back and took a deep breath as he laid his hands on his knees. He needed time to gather his wits and find stability. He closed his eyes and let the silence take him to a tranquil place. His nerves had calmed when he heard someone entering his space. His eyes peeled open and Antoinette was standing beside him in her gown. She gave him the once over before her eyes met his. Although her lips didn't move, his mind registered what her eyes were asking. He shook his head *no*, he hadn't bodied Malvo.

Antoinette left the living room and returned wearing latex gloves and toting a black trash bag. She helped her man pull off his blood splattered top, sweats and Timbs. She stuffed the items into the bag, tied it up and set it aside. She then took him by the hand and led him into the bathroom. She turned on the shower and helped him into the tub. She washed him up as he stood underneath the spray of the showerhead.

All of a sudden she broke down crying, bowing her head and sniffling. Her shoulders shook as she wept, tears dripping as quickly as she wiped them away.

Ronny turned the showerhead away from him. He ran his hand down his face, sweeping the access water away. The creases of his forehead deepened when he looked to his woman. He killed the shower water and kneeled down to her in the tub, tilting her chin up so they'd be at eye level.

"Baby, what's wrong?" He asked concerned. She was his queen and he wanted to do nothing more than to ease her pain. If she was hurting, then he was hurting ten times worse.

"I don't—I don't feel pretty anymore. Since the rape I've been feeling so ugly, babe."

"Awww, boo, you're pretty. You're the prettiest girl in the world." He hugged her to his wet chest and kissed the top of her head.

She pulled away and looked up into his face, eyes trickling wetness.

"You still think I'm pretty, really?" She asked with hopeful eyes.

"Yes, baby, I still think you're pretty." His sincerity dripped from his vocal cords.

"You don't think I'm disgusting?" He shook his head *no*. "Do you—do you still want me?" Her voice crackled and she sniffled.

"Always and forever." He told her.

A lone tear ran down her cheek but he swiped it away with his thumb before it could meet the floor. He then kissed her tenderly on the forehead.

"Prove it."

"How?" he asked, willing to do anything in order to make her feel as beautiful as he believed she was, inside and out.

"I want you to make love to me."

"Okay." He nodded, taking her by the chin and kissing her lips as if they were glazed with honey. "Let me dry off and I'ma take care of you."

Ronny dried off the front of his chest and arms while his lady tended to his back and legs. Once they were done, he took Antoinette by the hand and led her into the bedroom where they made passionate love. He didn't care about getting off, that night he only lived to please his woman in every sexual way imaginable. At the end of their escapade, Antoinette lay against his slightly hairy chest with a smirk on her face. He kissed her forehead and stared up at the ceiling with one hand behind his head.

I ain't gon' stop, mothafucka. You hear me? I ain't gon' stop until they're shoveling dirt onto your coffin. That's on everything I love. His last thoughts were of Malvo before he closed his eyes and drifted off to sleep.

*****

There was a full moon reining in the dark sky. All that could be heard besides crickets were the grunts of a man and a woman as they dug up the ground. Amazon and Ponytail were covered in smears of dirt. They took the time to stop and wipe their faces and foreheads with rags before stuffing them into their back pockets.

"Damn, did you have to kill the kid, though?" Amazon asked.

"I told her don't move, but she did." He scowled, switching the shovel to his other hand. "What do you want from me, huh?"

"I'm just saying, that's all," She went back to shoveling up dirt.

"Less saying and more digging," he spat with contempt.

"Kiss my ass." She spoke heatedly, smacking her butt.

"Suck it!" He grabbed the bulge in his pants. She gave him the middle finger. "Bah." He waved her off.

The Greek mobsters went about the task of digging more holes, three to be exact. Lying alongside a pile of dirt they'd dug was a short body wrapped up in black garbage bags. Once they were finished with the hole, Ponytail scooped up the body and dropped it down in the hole. He then pulled a flask from his back pocket and took a quick drink, before dousing the body with some of the alcohol.

"Ashes to ashes, dust to dust."

Tranay Adams

CHAPTER THREE

Fear looked over the orange pill bottle that contained the pain killers before popping the cap. He dumped one into the palm of his hand and threw it back. He then picked up the glass of water from the dresser and took a sip, washing it down. He kicked off his Timbs and lay back in bed, tucking a pillow behind his head. He'd just closed his eyes when the door opened and Eureka stepped in, pulling it shut behind her.

"How are you feeling?"

"I'm alright," he exhaled.

"I'm sorry that was a dumb ass question," she said, once she'd thought about it. The man had a gash in his stomach and his life's savings had been stolen. Of course he wasn't fine. She couldn't begin to imagine how he was feeling or what was going through his head. She couldn't help but to feel responsible. If she hadn't insisted on him letting her mother stay at his house, then shit wouldn't have went down like that. She could have kicked herself in the ass for the judgment call she made. It was foolish of her to think she could treat her mother like a regular person instead of someone with an illness.

Eureka pinched the bridge of her nose and shook her head. "I'm sorry, baby. I really am."

"I heard you the first couple of hundred times, Reka." He spoke with his eyes closed, tired of hearing her apologize. Her saying sorry wasn't making him feel better and it sure as shit wasn't going to bring back that safe.

"I know, boo." She straddled his body, coming face to face with him. He opened his eyes and saw a grin curling the end of her lips. He returned the gesture as she nuzzled her nose at the crease of his neck, giving him a hickey.

"Mmmm." He loved the feeling of her warm mouth sucking on his flesh. His chocolate hands curved around her waist and slipped her pants down around her ample bottom, revealing her black thong. He grabbed two big handfuls of her ass and booty meat seeped out between his fingers.

Eureka's tongue pierced between her lips and her head dipped, traveling along his collarbone and sliding up his neck. He hissed as she bit gently into the soft flesh underneath his chin, sucking on it as if it were a pregnant nipple ripe with milk.

"You like that, huh?" she questioned, feeling his steel press against her stomach as it rose to the occasion.

She slid down his torso and met his crotch, gently biting on his bulge through the jeans as she stared up at him seductively. She flashed him a naughty smile before she began unbuckling his belt and unbuttoning his jeans. She pulled them off and along came his boxer-briefs. Once the jeans had made it from over his dick, it jumped back up pulsating. His dick had curled up so high it was nearly touching his stomach. Eureka's cheeks puffed up as she hawked up saliva and spat on his joint. She watched her spit splatter against his meat and slide down. Before the white goo could meet his nut-sack, she grabbed his endowment by the shaft, stroking it up and down. She started off slowly at first and then she sped up causing his eyes to narrow and him to gasp. Her delicate touch felt exuberant to him. It made the veins in his cock bulge and caused the size of its head to double. His shit grew a little in width and length. She slowed her stroking and licked him underneath his shaft up to his helmet. She swirled her tongue around it and watched as his body shivered. She placed her mouth just at the head of the top of his member and sucked on it. He rasped and reached to push her head down further on his manhood, but she smacked his hand away.

"Uh uh," she shook her head no and wagged her finger. Her mouth engorged him. She guided her lips up and down his chocolate pole, spilling hot saliva down it and making all of those nasty sounds that drove him wild. She took him into the back of her throat and when he couldn't go any further, she pushed him in just a little more. She gagged some and veins appeared on her forehead and neck. She then hummed *Amazing Grace* and went back to tonguing him down. His big toes pointed while the other toes balled up. He clenched his ass cheeks and licked his lips. She was only giving him half of that juicy mouth but goddamn her head game was official.

He closed his eyes and clasped his hands behind his head. A smirk made an appearance on his face as he listened to her sucking, slurping, humming and moaning as if it were music playing on his headphones. When she stopped his eyelids peeled open to find her using her mouth to slide a condom down onto his meat. She got it on about half way before she rolled it down the rest of the way with her hands. She removed her top and peeled off her black thong, tossing them aside. She turned her back to him and kneeled. She grabbed his dick and eased down until his width filled the void between her legs.

Her head snapped back and she gasped when she'd gotten about halfway down, her warm juices flowing down his shaft. Once she had all of him up in her, she began working her hips with her pussy puking and regurgitating his meat. Fear grabbed a hold of each one of her buttocks controlling the pace she went. She had started riding him too fast. Although it felt good, he could feel himself about to bust off and he wanted to prolong the spectacular experience.

"Mmmm! Mmmm!" Her eyes were closed as she slowly rode him, feeling his pole massage her insides. From the sounds he was making she could tell he was enjoying it too. That turned her on. She wanted to know her man was enjoying their sexing as much as she was. He rubbed her ass and spanked each cheek, the slaps growing louder and harder each time his open palm met them. She hissed feeling the stings that brought her both pain and pleasure.

He slapped her one more time on her ass. "Hop off, baby." She fell off to the side of the bed and he got up. He stroked his cock with one hand while telling her how to lay with the other.

"Yeah, there you go, just like that." He grinned and nodded, appeased by the way she'd followed his instructions to the T. He stepped to the bed, snatching her to the edge of it and parting her legs. He held one up while she held the other. He smacked his steel against her swollen clit and slid it up and down the slit of her womanhood. Her pussy ran with her warm liquid and stained the sheet. A smirk came across his face as he watched her massage that tender flap of meat that was nestled between her southern lips. She couldn't wait to feel him all up in her. She was burning up, screaming to be fucked and he couldn't wait to oblige   her.

Having grown tired of the teasing, he drew his dick back and glided it into her pink wetness. She gasped feeling him slide inside of her treasure. He grabbed her other leg and held them both apart, gently thrusting in and out of her hole. Her nostril flared and she exhaled, feeling the head of him spearing her G-spot. He gave her half of him, then all of him. Going down in that thang deep to the end of his shaft and then pulling it back out to the tip. His strokes were slow and measured, and her small breasts jumped with each one that he delivered.

"Haa! Haa! Haa!" She breathed with her eyes closed, gripping the sheets. He went faster. Pushing his love in as far as it would go and pulling out, only to make another deposit. "Baby, don't—don't— don't stop." Her eyes rolled and she bit down on her bottom lip. He brought her small foot to his lips and his tongue made a cameo appearance. He licked her from the ball of her foot and up the arch. Discovering her toes, he sucked on the biggest one before moving to the second, the third, and then finally settling on them all.

"Mmmm," he said, mouthing on half of her foot while staring down at her pleasured face. He pampered the other foot as well, sucking hard on the ball of it. She massaged her breasts and squeezed her nipples, which were as hard as ever. He felt good, so good that her cum oozed around his girth looking like soap foam.

He held her feet together, going back and forth between licking and sucking on them

"Faster. Faster. Oooh. Faster." Her eyes went to their whites. Her nostrils grew even wider as she tightened her jaws. He opened her legs wide and pumped faster, showing that pussy who was boss and who it worked for.

Al Simpson, goddamn it, and don't you ever forget it.

"Ooooooh," her face contorted, forehead wrinkling as her lips puckered up. She massaged her breast with one hand and rubbed on her clit with the other, intensifying the sensual experience as he beat that mothafucking pussy up. He tilted his head back and closed his eyes as sweat cascaded down his face and back. He was diving in and out of her cunt, causing the bed to shift as he threw that dick.

His tongue hung out of his mouth like Michael Jordan as he held her by the bottoms of her foot and jabbed that pole of his in and out of her. He looked down watching his shit stoke her middle, causing her sex to ooze with its very own cream. He felt his loins growing sensitive with each stroke which meant he was about to shoot his load. His face morphed into something grotesque as he worked her feverishly. He threw his head back as sweat made his entire form glisten.

"Oooooooooh." She made that noise that let him know he was tearing it up.

"Uh—Uh—Uh—Shit—Awww, damn!" He talked that shit, staring up at the ceiling.

"Cum for me, baby. Bust that nut!" She hollered, stroking her swollen flap of meat faster, trying to get off one more time before he got his.

"Aww, shit. I'm cumming, I'm cumming, baby. Ahhhhh!" The tension released his body and fulfillment was painted across his face. His form jumped a couple of times having just unleashed a mean ass nut. He fell over on to the bed beside Eureka panting out of breath. "Goddamn, a nigga needed that, good looking out, boo."

"Shit, I should be thanking you." She scooted her ass up against his flaccid meat and drew his arm around her waist. He kissed the back of her neck and behind her ears, which caused her to giggle because she was ticklish. He smirked, thinking of how childlike she was.

Their bodies were hot and sticky, but they didn't mind because there wasn't any place they would rather be than wrapped up in one another's arms. Fear placed tender kisses up Eureka's spine as she grew quiet and still, thinking.

"Babe," she began.

"Yeah," he answered between kisses.

"What's going to happen should you ever run into my   mother?"

His kisses abruptly stopped. He pressed his forehead against the back of her head and exhaled, thinking on it.

"I don't know what to tell you, Reka. Your mother stole every cent I had. You know the caliber of nigga I am. That's an offense punishable by death." When he said that, she turned around to face him sporting a disturbed expression.

"Fear, are you telling me that you're going to kill my mother?" She looked deeply into his eyes, trying to see if she could gage what was on his mind but she couldn't. He was good at hiding his feelings. You wouldn't know where his head was unless he told you.

"No," he answered. "I'm telling you I don't know what's going to happen should we ever cross paths. That's all I've got to give you right now, so I hope it's enough. Let's worry about your mother when the time comes, okay?" Her eyes wondered away from his and he lifted her chin with a curled finger. Their eyes had a reunion.

"Okay?" she nodded *yes* and he kissed her lovingly.

"Come on, I need to shower." He took her hand and led her into the bathroom.

*****

"Anyway, I figure Thursday night we hit this nigga, Arkane." Fear passed Eureka the loofah so she could wash his back. "What chu think?"

"Let's do it."

"Alright then, Thursday night it is."

He turned his back to her, allowing the spray of water to hit his face and chest, rinsing off the soap. She took the loofah and was about to wash his back when she noticed the welts from a whipping he'd gotten some time ago. Not feeling the loofah hit his back yet, Fear turned around raising an eyebrow. The expression on her face told him she was curious as to why he'd allowed himself to be beaten so brutally. She remembered seeing the welts that night in the garage when he'd given Constance a lashing. Although she did admire him for not holding himself above his law, she couldn't help but wonder what he'd done to feel he'd deserve to be scarred for life.

Fear placed his hands flat on the tiled wall and hung his head, letting the water beat down on the top of his scalp and roll off of his face. He closed his eyes and licked his lips. "Wash my back and I'll tell you how I got them."

She shook her head *no.* "No. It's cool. You don't have—

"It's alright. I know you're curious as to how and I'm in the mood to tell." He told her, eyes still closed. Eureka began lathering his back with the loofah as he started to tell the tale of how he'd earned his scars.

Fear was called upon to gather intelligence on a mafia wise guy by the name of Mickey Carbone. Mickey was rumored to be carrying on an affair with the wife of his boss. For the next two weeks the killer kept his charge under surveillance. He gathered more than enough photographic evidence to prove that the capo was indeed stepping out with his boss's wife. When he brought said photos to his client's attention, he immediately ordered the executions of his wife and his successor.

Fear caught up with the adulteress and done away with her with ease, two to the back of the cranium put her to sleep for an eternity. With her out of the way, he set his sights on old Mickey. But when the man next to the man caught wind that his fuck-buddy had met with the grave, he tucked his tail and ran out of state. It took a while but Fear was finally able to locate him.

Fear picked the backdoor lock and quietly pushed his way inside. He closed the door back gently and pulled out his .9mm automatic with the silencer attached. Sliding the Scream movie ghost-mask over his face, he crept through the kitchen and into the dimly lit living room where he heard the television going. As soon as his head peeked inside of the doorway, he saw the back of someone's head while they were watching TV. He smiled behind the mask thinking of how the poor bastard wasn't expecting his demise. With footsteps as soft as cotton, he advanced through the room. His movement's fluid and his heart beat amped as he gripped the handle of his weapon tighter. He would never be such a coward as to shoot a man in the back. That wasn't respectable. See, he wanted all of his victims to see his eyes before he gave them that heat.

Banger extended at the back of Mickey's head, the killer moved counter clockwise around the couch. When he was at an angle, his eyes widened. It wasn't Mickey that was there but a model head with a blonde wig on it sitting on a stack of pillows and facing the TV. The blue illumination from the television danced on the model head. A grunt at his rear prompt him to turn around but before he could he felt sharp metal slam into his back. He whipped around and found Mickey looking from a bent butcher's knife to him. The Italian mobster threw down the butcher's knife and rushed the killer. Fear lifted his .9mm but before he could send him to the cloudy skies above he was tackled. The men fell on the floor rolling around as they struggled over   control   of   the   gun.

"You thought I didn't see your ass creeping toward my house, did you?" Mickey gritted his teeth as his head shook. Hands clutching the .9mm, he pushed the gun toward Fear's face. Veins formed on his forehead and neck as he settled his finger on the trigger. He was just about to pull it when a sharp pain shot through his crotch causing his face to ball up in agony. He lost control of the banger and fell to the floor, clutching his cock and balls.

Fear scrambled to his feet and pointed his gun at his face. He turned his head as he held a hand just above the weapon to shield him from blood splatter. Hearing movement at his back, he swung around and squeezed off. Choot! The little dark haired boy's eyes shot open as well as his mouth. A red dot quickly expanded at the center of his pajama shirt as he collapsed where he stood.

"Noooooooo!" Fear and Mickey said in unison. The hit man and the father watched the boy fall three times in slow motion, real dramatic like. Mickey scrambled over to his son as he lay bleeding on the kitchen floor gasping for air. Fear was in a trance after what he'd done. He staggered back and plopped down on the couch. He was wide eyed staring at nothing with his mouth stuck open, gripping his gun. The horrified cries over his shoulder brought him around and he found Mickey, hunched over his son. His cheeks were wet with tears and he was making an ugly   face.

"No, not my boy, not my baby boy." Mickey cried

his eyes out, snot dripping from his nose. The devastation he wore told the story of a man that had been shot through the heart with an arrow. "Oh, why, father? Why my Jonathan?" He croaked, holding his limp son's head against his chest for a time. Thinking that he'd best call 9-1-1 before it was too late. He lay his son back down on the linoleum and kissed him on the forehead. Fear watched as he came up from off of the floor and retrieved the cordless phone.

Seeing a future behind bars if that call was made, the killer sprang into action and pulled the trigger. A black hole the size of a nickel opened on Mickey's forehead and a crimson splatter came from the back of his skull as the hushed bullet made its exit. His eyes stared ahead at nothing. He fell to the linoleum right after the cordless white telephone with speckles of blood did. Fear walked upon him, looking him over before he deposited two into his sternum. He then kneeled down to the little boy as he stared up at the ceiling, mouth agape. He placed two fingers to his neck and found that his pulse had expired. He hung his head and massaged the bridge of his nose.

"Goddamn," he cursed himself. "God—damn you." He exhaled. With a sweep of his gloved hand he shut the kid's   eyes.

With his business concluded he left the house with the murder of an innocent child on his conscience. It was just one more thing he would have to answer for on Judgment day.

"You want me to kill you?" Constance frowned as she took the gun from Fear. She looked at him like he had shit sliding down his face.

"Yes. I want you to shoot me in my head." He repeated, hooking his thumbs in the loops of his jeans and *staring her dead in the eyes. He was prepared to meet his fate head on without so much as blinking.*

"You're crazy. No." She shook her head no and sat the banger down on the kitchen table. "I won't do it."

"What chu mean you won't do it?" he asked angrily. "I killed an innocent child. I. Took. His. Life." He took his time saying each word so they would resonate with her. "I broke the law. You kill an innocent person and you shall be sentenced to death. You read the book. Laws are not to be broken, and if they are violators should be persecuted. No one is ... "

"Above L.O.E, not even you." She finished what he was saying. "I know that. And what happened that night was clearly an accident. You didn't mean to kill that kid."

He shook his head. "It doesn't matter."

"It does to me." She shot back. "I'm not going to kill you, and that's final."

"Constance!" he barked with authority.

She folded her arms across her chest and switched her weight to her other foot. "No."

"Goddamn you, Constance! You pick up that fucking gun right now, or so help me I'll shoot chu in the face!" When she didn't budge, he snatched his banger off of his waist and pointed it at her. "Oh, you think I'm playing?"

"Oh, I don't doubt that you're serious. I wouldn't dare call your bluff." She told him with glassy eyes threatening to drip tears. "But If I kill you, I may as well kill myself soon after 'cause I'm only living for you. I don't have anyone else. It's you and I against the world, remember? That's what you told me the day after my training."

Fear's face tightened as he mad dogged her and bit down hard at the corner of his bottom lip. He gripped his gun tighter and added a little more pressure to the trigger. They were locked into one another gaze. Hers said she was ready to die and his said he was ready to kill. Fear knew he could drop his protégé right then without batting an eye, but to do so would be dead wrong. Constance hadn't done anything so it would be selfish for him to sentence them both to death.

"Arghhhh! Fuck! Fuck! Fuck!" Furious, he began beating himself upside the head with the .9mm until he opened up a gash and burgundy blood trickled down. He dropped to the floor bawling with his knees against his chest. She got down on her knees beside him. She held his head against her chest and caressed his head. "I killed him, I killed that little boy! Oh, God, what have I done? What have I done?" His eyes squeezed shut and his mouth hung open as he hollered and his body shuddered.

"Shhhhhh, it's going to be okay." She slowly took the gun from him, setting it aside on the floor. She kissed the top of his head and rubbed his back. He wrapped his arms around her and she tightened her embrace, comforting him.

About twenty minutes later, Fear came to his senses and rose to his feet. He took Constance's hand and pulled her to stand.

"Accident or no accident, I must be punished for what I did last night."

"Fear, you..."

"Shhhhhh." He hushed her with a finger to his lips. "Regardless of what you say, I will answer for what I have done."

*****

"Twenty five lashings." Fear told Eureka. "I blacked out from the pain before I reached fifteen. I didn't even feel the last ten." He shook his head. "My back was so raw I had to sleep on my stomach for a month."

"How old was he?"

"Who?"

"The boy."

"Fifteen," he answered. "Same age as Anton."

"Is that why you've taken to him?" she asked. "You're trying to redeem yourself for the life you've took?"

"In a fucked up sense, yes." He conceded. "Although I am teaching the lil' homie all of the right ways to do the wrong things, I'm still preparing him for what awaits him in this game. So, in a way, I'm still preserving life. Depending on how you look at it."

Eureka nodded her understanding.

"You done back there?"

"Yeah."

Fear rinsed the soap off of his back and then went on to wash her up.

CHAPTER FOUR
One Night Later…

The night was cold and windy with loose trash being blown down the sidewalk and streets. Malvo threw open the front passenger door of his truck and jumped down onto the asphalt. He gave his surroundings the once over as he took a pull from a withering cigarette. Smoke wafted from his nostrils and mouth, blowing away with the wind. He dropped the cigarette on the ground and mashed it out underneath his Timberland boot. He slammed the SUV's door shut and stuck his hands inside of his leather jacket. He stepped upon the curb and journeyed down the sidewalk. He walked a few feet until he came upon a telephone booth. He rested his arm on top of the telephone booth. Looking about, he ran a hand down his face and massaged his chin. He looked up the block and saw an old wino wearing a blue bubble coat with the stuffing hanging out of it. He clutched a brown paper bag that concealed a bottle of cheap booze. The closer the man drew the more of his stench Malvo took in, which caused his forehead to wrinkle and his nose to scrunch up. The old wino stopped a couple of feet away from Malvo. He eyed him suspiciously as he twisted the cap off of whatever he had in the brown paper bag and took it to the head. After a long guzzle, the old wino twisted the cap back on his bottle and wiped his mouth with the back of his hand and belched. Malvo turned his head after getting a whiff of the foul odor. The old wino stopped before him, his head moving about lazily as if it would fall off of his neck.

"Say—say, young brotha. You wouldn't happen to have fifty cents, now would ya?" he asked, looking like he would tip over and fall any minute.

"Gon' about your business, bruh," Malvo spat on the sidewalk and glanced at his titanium Rolex.

"Say what?"

Malvo looked him directly in the eyes and spoke slowly. "Get. The. Fuck. Out. Of. Here."

"Ah, come on, man. I just need two…" The old wino was cut short when Malvo lifted his T-shirt exposing the banger on his waist. The wino's eyes grew as big as saucers and his mouth dropped open. "Oooooooh," he said like a child in class seeing one of the other kids doing something they shouldn't have been doing.

"Bounce, nigga."

"Okay. I'm going." He moved along, holding up his hand and the bottle of cheap liquor. The sight of the banger seemed to make him as sober as a judge.

"Gon', lil' funky mothafucka," Malvo followed behind him hostilely, talking shit. "Beat the street, nigga." He kicked him in the ass pitching him forward causing him to lose his footing, crashing to the sidewalk. The bottle cracked inside of the brown paper bag soaking it and turning it an even darker brown. Malvo came up behind him, drawing his banger and kicking him in the ass. He fell to the sidewalk again and hurriedly got back to his feet, sprinting up the block as if he was at football practice. Malvo laughed heartily seeing the old wino go, he needed a laugh after all of the shit he had been through the past few weeks. He tucked his banger back on his waist and posted back up beside the telephone booth. He looked to his truck and saw Crunch shaking his head at what had just occurred. He waved him off and smacked his lips. He then pulled out his cell phone and punched in some numbers. "Let me see where the fuck this nigga at, man."

As Malvo was punching numbers into the cell phone the shadows behind him began to stir and a dread headed man in a brown duster stepped forth. Malvo had just placed the cell phone to his ear when a leather gloved hand snaked around his neck, placing a machete almost as big as a small sword against his Adams apple. His body stiffened and his eyes bulged, he slowly lifted the cell phone. He wanted to swallow his spit but the machete was pressed so hard against his neck he thought he'd slice his own throat if he did. The dread head took the cell phone and tossed it over his shoulder. He then pulled Malvo back into the alley by the collar of his leather jacket until the darkness swallowed them. He shoved him up against the wall inside of the alley and snatched his banger off of his waist, stashing it on his own person. He then lifted up his shirt and felt down his back and around his pants legs. Malvo frowned as he watched him going about the task wondering what the hell he was doing. He was checking to see if he wearing a wire and had any other weapons.

"How did you get into contact with me?" When the dread head spoke he sounded like he was speaking through a voice distorter device. Malvo peered closely but he could only make out part of his face thanks to the darkness. "Do you hear me talking to you?"

Malvo nodded his understanding. "A mutual friend gave me your contact info."

"Alright then." The dread head took a step back, still holding the machete against his throat in case he tried to pull a fast one.

"There's a photograph inside of my jacket."

The dread stuck his hand inside of the leather jacket and pulled out a folded photograph. He unfolded the photograph, looked over it and back up into Malvo's eyes. "The whole family?"

"No, just the girl."

"Gimmie the rundown."

"As of now, I don't have shit," Malvo admitted. "I was told you're the cat to see to find people and make them disappear."

"This girl is just a kid. I don't murder children." The dread head dropped the photograph to the ground and turned around sheathing his machete as he made to leave the   alley.

"Nah, she's nineteen and I don't want you to kill her." He picked the photograph back up. "I want chu to bring her to me."

"Right." The dread head replied without turning around. "You want me to bring her to you so you can kill her." When he didn't respond, he went on to say, "That's exactly what I thought."

"Wait, I'll give you 30K." When the dread head kept it moving, he kept rattling off numbers until he dropped one that got him to stop in his track. "One hundred thousand dollars." The killer turned around slowly and a shady smirk formed on the dope man's lips. "I thought that may   get   your   attention."

"If you're fucking with me, I'm going to cut chu every way but loose."

*****

Crunch was sitting behind the wheel keeping an eye on Malvo when his cell phone rung and vibrated. He looked at the screen and saw his grandmother's face and name; a grin came across his lips.

"Hey, grand ma?" he spoke into his cell. "Yeah, I know it's getting late—" he stole a glance at the digital clock in the dashboard. "—Nah, I've already eaten. Okay. I should be back home within an hour or so. Alright, I love you, too." He disconnected the call. When he looked up worry lines came across his forehead; Malvo had vanished.

*****

"I'm not fucking around here. I'm talking square business, no whammies."

"I want half up front."

"Not a fucking chance." Malvo shot back. "How I am supposed to know that you won't take my money and run off with it."

"How do I know you won't keep it once the job is done?"

Malvo shrugged, "You're a contract killa, find me and blow my fucking brains out."

The dread head looked away massaging his chin. "You've gotta deal, but if you fuck me on this, they'll never be able to tell the difference from you and a slab off beef hanging up in a meat locker."

"Fair enough," Malvo said. "Oh, something else." He reached inside of his jacket and pulled out a slip of paper, handing it to the hit man. "I want chu to dig up every address on this cat as well as everyone of his living relatives."

"Are you telling me what to do or are you requesting this of me?"

"It's a request." He tossed him a roll of *real* money secured by a rubber band. He examined the roll before tucking it into the pocket of his trench coat.

"I'll be back with you in less than twenty-four hours."

"Thank you."

"Malvo!" Crunch called out. When Malvo turned around he found him at the end of the alley with a gun in his   hand.

"Yeah?" He called back out.

"You alright?"

"I'm straight." When Malvo turned back around the dreadlock rocking assassin had vanished. The only thing left in his place was a thick fog.

"Hmmm." Malvo turned back around, sticking his hands in the pockets of his jacket. He walked off down the alley where Crunch was standing.

Eureka hadn't a clue but her life had just been put on a countdown.

*****

Cling! Clank! Clang!

The metals clasped as the chain yanked back and forth with Giselle trying to get away. She tried spitting on her wrist and even vomiting on it to slicken it, hoping she'd be able to slip her hand out of the shackle but there wasn't any use. Exhausted, she dropped to the floor on her ass. She looked around for anything she could possibly use to free herself from the restraint, but she couldn't find anything. Giselle was as sick as a goddamn dog. It had been a while since she had herself some dope and her stomach was cramping something awful. She knew at the rate she was going, with her declining health and all, she'd surely be stinking up the room as a corpse in the next couple of days.

Suddenly an idea went through her head like an arrow and she snapped her fingers. She kicked off her right Timberland boot and pulled off her filthy, holey sock. She rolled the sock up and stuffed it into her mouth biting down as hard as she could. Keeping her shackled hand as close to the ground as she could, she squeezed her eyes closed and tried to build the courage for what she was about to attempt. Her chest heaved and her nostrils flared as she built up the tolerance for pain. Her eyes snapped open and she screamed with the sock muffling the sound.

Crack! Crack!

"Ahhhhh!" she hollered in agony as she stomped on the bone that joined her wrist and thumb, hearing it crackling and breaking scared her but she had to keep going for her shot at freedom.

Crack! Crackk! Crackkk!

"Aghhhh!"

The bone's breaking sounded like Kibbles and Bits dog food being crushed. She glanced down at her mangled hand, it was totally disfigured. Tears spilling down her cheeks, she tried to pull her wrist free but the bone hadn't broken enough. She figured with a few more stomps she'd be able to finally pull her wrist loose. She took a couple of deep breaths and wailed like a mad woman, eyes bulging with a crazed look in her pupils.

Crack! Crack! Crack!

The bone broke into her palm making it look like she only had four fingers. Hunched over, she yanked her hand as hard as she could. Her wrist slipped out of the shackle and she stumbled back hastily, landing on her back. Lying on her back, she looked at her broken hand. It was bloody and deformed like she'd been born with it that way. She sobbed hard, the pain was horrific but finally she was free. She pulled the sock out of her mouth and tied her hand up as tightly as she could with it. She then stuffed her bare foot into her Timberland boot and dashed out of the boiler room.

Giselle crept over to the iron door. She gently pulled it open but the further it did, the louder the noise it made. *Shit,* she thought to herself as she looked up and down the dimly lit corridor. The hallway was littered with loose trash, cobwebs hung from the ceiling and the occasional rat would scurry past. Giselle crept out one foot at a time, keeping a close eye on things. She didn't know where Constance was but she had a feeling she was nearby. She could just feel it. It was something in her gut that told her so. She let the iron door get as close to the lock as she could so it wouldn't make much noise before letting it go. Big mistake, when the door met the lock it made a loud metal click. That sound swept throughout the length of the corridor and she was sure that someone had heard it.

Grrrrr! Grrrrr!

The growls of twin hounds poisoned Giselle heart with terror. She swallowed spit. Eyes wide, lips peeled. Her face shiny and dirty making her look like a runaway slave. A panicked expression painted her face as her head snapped back and forth up the hallway, cradling her broke and throbbing hand. She froze where she was with her eyes narrowing into slits as she strained to peer through the darkness. She heard the slight foot falls as four of something moved forth, stirring movement within the shadows. Her neck coiled when she saw four red orbs approaching. She held up her hand and took a couple steps backwards. That's when they made themselves visible, twin big head Rottweiler's with flinching upper lips, baring their fangs. Saliva dripping from their mouths like raindrops. They snarled and snapped at Giselle, ready to make her their next meal.

"Oh, shit!"

Giselle spun around and hauled ass in the opposite direction with the vicious beasts snapping at her heels. She was running so hard she felt her heels kicking her in the ass as she made her way down the corridor.

Woof! Woof!

The dogs were on her like stink on shit. For as fast as she was running, they were running that much faster. Her lungs ignited, catching on fire. She could feel them burning inside of her chest. As bad as she wanted to stop to take a breather she knew she couldn't because that would be her undoing. All she could do was tilt her head up every so often and take gulps of air. Another film of sweat masked her face. As quick as the beads of sweat formed on her forehead they were blown away with the wind blowing against her as she made hurried steps.

Haa! Haa! Haa! Haa! Haa! Haa!

She huffed and puffed. She slowed to a jog when she reached the foyer, head darting all around looking for an escape. While she was doing this, she was none the wiser to the dark figure that had emerged over her head upon the long thick pipe. Clutching a black pipe, the figure folded its arms across its chest and watched its prisoner move like a lab rat in a maze. Giselle dashed over to double doors and tried to yank it open, causing the chains securing it to rattle. She was in such a panic she didn't even notice the doors were locked up.

Woof! Woof!

Giselle swung around with her heart about to leap out of her chest. Her shit was beating so hard it looked like it was trying to punch its way out of her chest cavity. Breathing heavily, she took in the full scope of her surroundings. When she spotted an unchained door to her left with a light flashing beneath it as a car was driving by, she darted for it with the dogs running on each side of her snapping.

"Arghhh!" She hollered and grabbed her thigh as one of the beast bit into her flesh. She hobbled along as fast as she could until the other one jumped on her back biting at it. She tried to swat it away and he bit her hand. "Ahhh!" The first one bit down on the sleeve of her hoodie, whipping its head from left to right as it pulled.

"Evil, Terror, get your asses back, now!" A voice rang out. And just like that, the ferocious hounds converted to pups under the thunderous authority of their master. They stepped aside and allowed their owner a path to a weeping Giselle as she clutched her wounded leg. "You tried to run, huh? You can't escape hell, baby. You've gotta be set free. It takes humongous balls to do what you did to get free, either that or desperate measures are a mothafucka." She spit off to the side and continued. "You're probably thinking how do I know this right? Well, that's easy. There are cameras everywhere in this place." She pointed to all of the cameras within the building with her pipe. Giselle looked everywhere the pipe was pointed and saw a small red light which belonged to surveillance cameras. "Uh huh, now the punishment for trying to escape." She pressed her boot against her leg, pinning it to the ground. Lifting the pipe above her head, she swung it with all of her might against her ankle.

Crack!

Her foot twisted in the opposite direction, snapping. Giselle gasps as her eyes turned to their whites and her mouth snapped open. She attempted to scream but before she could she descended into darkness.

Constance grabbed Giselle by her good ankle and dragged her back toward her prison. She walked along whistling with her hounds following behind her, wagging their tails and playing around with one another. The hit woman made her prisoner a homemade splint for her foot and shackled her wrist once again. She wouldn't be escaping this time.

*****

Fifteen hours later…

Just like the dread head said, he got back with Malvo in less than twenty-four hours with the information he required. Siska didn't have that many living relatives to speak of, not in the United States at least. Out here he had a much younger sister and her eighteen year old son by the name of Bon.

Malvo turned over the photograph of Bon from the side that the address was written on. He was a dorky looking kid with a shaved head and specs and a grill covered by braces. An evil smile spread across Malvo's face as his plump fingers caressed the photo he was given. The young man would make the perfect sacrificial lamb. He wasn't exactly Siska's kid but he was as close to it as he was going to get, so he'd do for now.

An hour later

Boom!

The front door flew open and a chunk of its frame went hurling across the room. The loud crash startled Bon where he was on the couch playing his PS4 and smoking a joint. He jumped up from the couch and took off, tripping and falling over himself but getting right back up. A masked up Malvo and Crunch jetted after him, gripping them thangs.

"Come here, mothafucka!" Malvo yelled after him.

Bon had just unlocked the door and pulled it opened when something hard swept across the back of his shaved head. "Ooof!" He winced, falling off to the side into the corner of the back porch beside the washing machine. He looked up and saw a masked Crunch clutching his ratchet as he kicked and stomped on him. All he saw were white flashes with each assault and before he knew it he'd grown dizzy. His eye was threatening to shut and his lips were busted and bleeding.

"Grab him!" Malvo hollered, snatching Bon by his limp wrist. "Grab his other arm so we drag him in the bathroom.

Ten minutes later...

Bon's handcuffed wrists hung over the neck of the showerhead. Malvo slipped on a pair of black leather weight lifting gloves. He looked to Crunch who was standing near the sink with Siska on Face-Time so he could watch the show live through the young man's cell phone. Crunch gave him a nod which let him know he was recording. Malvo cracked the knuckles on both of his hands and went to work on the kid. The first punch to the gut knocked the wind out of him, making his eyes bug and he mouth shoot open. The second shot to the gut made him wince and grumble in agony. From there Malvo worked that ass over beating the youngster like he was a slab of meat and he was Stallone in Rocky.

When he was done the boy was slumped on the neck of the showerhead with his knees bending. The side of his face was swollen as well as his nose and lips. Blood bubbled in his mouth and dripped out into the tub. His face and chest was slickened red from the beating. Bon looked like he'd experienced the worse day of his life. The only indication he was still alive was the twitching of his one good eye and his moaning in pain.

Malvo stepped out of the tub breathing like a raging bull with speckles of blood on his face. He picked up his burner from off of the sink and pressed it against his temple. He turned his murderous eyes toward the cell phone Crunch was holding.

"Don't do it! Don't chu dare do it, you motherfucker!" Siska bellowed. And while he was hollering, Malvo was looking back and forth between the cell and Bon, still holding the gun to his dome. Bon slowly lifted his head. His eyes shot to their corners seeing the big man holding steel to it. His eyes bled with terror and his busted lips trembled.

"Nooooooo!" Bon tilted his head back and screamed aloud.

"Malvooooooo!" Siska screamed with spit flying from his lips.

Malvo squeezed his eyes closed.

Blocka!

Chunks of brain and blood splattered against the tiled walls of the shower and against the side of Malvo's face. The blood flew everywhere and speckle of it clung to the screen of the cell phone distorting Siska's image. Malvo took the cell phone from Crunch. Siska had his head hung and was massaging the bridge of his nose.

"Look at me, old man! Look at me," he pulled the ski-mask up just above his eyebrows. The Greek mobster looked up with a pair of glassy eyes displaying his hurt. "I did this to you! Me!" He pointed to his chest with his gun. "Meeee!" He shouted.

Siska's face transformed with anger and his jaws throbbed as he gritted. He stared at Malvo for a time, quietly   seething.

"You're a dead man," he said before disconnecting the call.

Now you get to feel my pain, Malvo thought of the Greek crime lord's loss as he headed out of the bathroom with Crunch following closely behind.

Tranay Adams

CHAPTER FIVE

Thursday night…

The sun set and darkness blossomed like a daisy in the summer. It was 8:30 PM and the wolves were out in the night hunting, looking for something to quench their thirst. And what best to hydrate them than blood? Halfway down the street was a little Mexican food stand that prohibited you to dine outside. It was well lit and had chairs sitting at tables that had large umbrellas standing out of them to keep the customers shaded from the hot sun. Customers were coming to and from the establishment with greasy brown paper bags. Unbeknownst them, hidden within the recesses of the darkness were the wolves and they couldn't wait for a drink.

"Is that him?" Anton asked as he commanded the van down the residential block.

"Yeah, that's his bitch-ass," Fear confirmed, looking over his shoulder through the windshield, holding a choppa. They called them boys choppas because they chopped niggaz down like a lawn mower when they got busy.

"How you won't me to play it?" Anton asked in a hushed tone as if someone would hear him.

"Kill the lights and creep 'em. We 'bout to wet all of these pussies, real life." He loaded the last copper missile shaped bullet into the slot of his assault rifle. He looked up and saw Eureka ejecting the magazine into her M-16 rifle. She looked sexier than a mothafucka in that moment. It was nothing he loved more than a gangster-ass bitch. Lowering his choppa, he stepped to her and grabbed the back of her neck. He pulled her close and tilted his head to the side as he opened his mouth. Their lips mashed together and their tongues seeped out, discovering one another's mouths as they kissed sloppily. He pulled back and wiped the extra spit from the corner of her mouth with his thumb. She smiled and pecked his lips one last time.

"You alright, ma?"

"I'm gucci. Let's give these niggaz an invitation to the next life."

"Ant, get as close as you can up on 'em."

"Got chu, big homie."

Anton eased up on the crowd of men as Eureka grabbed the handle of the door and gently began to slide it open. They got about ten feet upon Arkane and his henchmen before the van's door was thrown open. Their assault rifles emerged and the henchmen's eyes lit up and their mouths widen. They all reached for their guns which were tucked on their waists but before they could clear them, rapid gunfire consumed the night's air.

*****

The West Coast Connection had taken the liberty to beef up their security since their falling out with Fear. The bosses were on high alert and although they had money and guns on their side, they were well aware of how the killer got down. He moved calmly and calculated with the quickness of lightening and the impact of thunder. And by the time someone realized what was happening, they'd already be dead.

Arkane rose from the table where he was shaded by an umbrella having finished off his last greasy taco. He wiped off his hands and dropped the balled up napkin onto his paper plate. Picking up his soda, he took a sip from his straw and his henchmen formed around him. He moved within the ring of bodies as they escorted him to his car which was parked across the street. Hearing his cell phone ring with the music he'd programmed for the new chick he bagged at the Rodeo, he pulled it off of his hip.

I got hoes/I got hoes/ in different area (area)/area (codes)

His lips curled into a smile as he pressed *answer* and pressed the cell to his ear.

"What's up, redbone?" He spoke into his phone.

"Heyyy, boo, how are—

Rat! Tat! Tat! Tat! Tat! Tat! Tat! Tat!

Pat! Pat! Pat! Pat! Pat! Pat! Pat! Pat!

"Arghhh!"

"Ahhh!"

"Gahhh!"

Golden orange flashes of light went off as the assault rifles spat hard and rapidly. The henchmen hollered out in agony as their flesh was chewed up before they could draw their guns. Blood rained on the cracked sidewalk and gun smoke wafted in the air. Everyone crumpled to the ground and the van sped away.

Arkane grimaced as he lay on his side looking around at all of the black hole riddled crimson bodies strewn around him. His left arm was nearly severed from the onslaught of sharp bullets. It dangled off to the side hanging on by a pinch of skin. The hand of his mangled arm was dragged across the sidewalk as he crawled into the street with his good arm, groaning. Hearing a car speeding in his direction, he turned his head and was blinded by the blaring headlights of a van—the van carrying the shooters. He made to move faster but to no avail.

Bumppp!

The van ran over Arkane's body causing it to tumble along the street. *Urrrrk.* The van came to a halt.

His head bobbled as he looked up, nose and mouth bloody. He made a funny gagging noise as he choked on his own blood, looking up at the headlights of the van. His eyes narrowed as the twin bright blinding circles shined on his face. He wanted to roll out of the way but he was fucked with a capital *F.* His body had been horribly crippled from the van running over him.

*****

Fear slid into the driver seat, shifted the gear into drive and revved up the engine. His head slightly tilted down as he mad dogged Akrane through the windshield and smiled sinisterly. He lifted his foot off of the brake pedal and mashed the gas pedal to the floor. The van took off speeding, barreling toward the crippled drug dealer.

"No, nigga, fuck you!" Fear spat, remembering their encounter back at the restaurant.

"Ahhhhhh!" Arkane blared, right before his head burst like a rotten water melon when the van's tire crushed it and dragging him up the street. A half of a block later the tire released his head and sped off.

*****

Crunch lay in bed in a wife beater and boxers, laughing his ass off at Tom & Jerry. Hearing his cell phone ring and vibrate, he looked to the dresser to see it dancing about. He narrowed his eyes as he looked closely at the lit screen, trying to see if his eyes were playing tricks on him.

He picked up the remote control and muted the TV. Tossing the remote aside, he answered his cell and placed it to his ear.

"What's cracking, Ronny?"

"You tell me, you bitch ass nigga."

Crunch sat up in bed laughing. He took the time to light up the blunt he was smoking earlier. "Now, you and I both know that bitch doesn't pump through these veins. You know how I give it up, you seen me in action, nigga. Respect my gangsta."

For a moment there was silence as Ronny thought over what he'd been told. Crunch was right. He was an official nigga and his murder game was off the chain. There wasn't a man and/or thing he was afraid of.

"I never thought I'd live to see the day that my dawg turned on me."

"Turn on you? Mothafucka you the one that ran off with Malvo's shit." He shot back. "What? You thought that there wasn't gonna be any consequences behind that? I strapped up and rolled out. Would have done the same thang for you had the shoe been on the other foot."

"Boy, has he pulled the wool over your eyes."

Crunch blew smoke out into the air. "Fuck you talking about?"

"The money he sent me to cop with was fake."

Crunch's brow furrowed, "Bullshit. I reject your deposit."

"Oh, really?"

Ronny gave Crunch the rundown on what had occurred when he went to make the drop. He included how he was chained up and beaten inside of the chop shop and the near death experience down in the basement. When he was finished he had his once right-hand man having second thoughts about his boss. But still he wasn't for sure and he needed proof.

As far as Crunch knew Malvo had just begun running the scam with the fake money. He found it hard to believe he'd chance sending him or Ronny on a trip with the counterfeit bills to make an exchange. It would be too risky. There would be a chance of one of them never coming back alive. He knew Malvo was as scandalous as they come but he couldn't see him playing one of his boys like that.

Nah, that nigga Ronny running G, Crunch thought. *Why in the fuck would Malvo do some foul shit like that? Homie been knowing us since we were knee high to a caterpillar. He's like our father and shit.*

"How do I know you aren't just making this shit up?"

"Proof. The next time he has you go to make a drop see if the money is authentic. Buy one of those markers they use to check to see if currency is real. You can get one from Office Depot or Staples." While he was talking, Crunch was jotting down the names of the stores and what kind of pen to purchase.

"Also, the money will more than likely have blue rubber-bands around it. I think that's how he separates the real from the fake."

"If what you're saying is true, then what?"

You hate yourself 'cause you realize you betrayed your only friend in this God forsaken world." Crunch closed his eyes for a moment and peeled them back open. He'd thought about what he'd been told. "Afterwards, you call me and we get in the streets with them toys and play." Silence fell as both men were left with his own thoughts. Moments later that silence was broken. "Crunch?"

"Yeah."

"You broke my heart." Ronny said from the opposite end, gripping the telephone so tightly that his knuckles shown. His face was twisted into a scowl and his eyes were attempting to drip tears. He squeezed his eyes closed and dried the wetness. *Clang!* He slammed the telephone down on the receiver and walked away.

*****

"Alright, family, dump this bitch." Fear told Anton, holding out his fist.

"I gotchu." Anton dapped him up.

"As soon as you're done, call me so that I can pick you up," Eureka said, sounding like someone's mother as she leaned over into the front seat.

"I told y'all you don't have anything to worry about. I got this." Anton looked between them both as he assured   them.

"That's what I'm talking about." Fear pulled the drawstrings of the sack, closing the assault rifles that they'd used that night inside. He then laid them across his lap and dapped up his little homie. After he slammed the door shut, he ducked back down inside of the window. "Alright, G, you be careful out there."

"All the time," Anton replied.

Fear tapped the top of the van and started for the house, pulling his keys from out of his pocket.

"Alright now, I love you."

"I love you too, sis." She hugged him with one arm, pulling him closer and kissing him on the forehead.

Eureka hopped out of the van and tucked her hands into her jacket pocket as she walked toward the house. Crossing the threshold, she saw the golden illumination of the fireplace as well as it warmth as it logs roasted. Fear was on his knees wearing his boxer-briefs and Timbs. He'd just folded up the clothes he'd worn that night and was placing them inside of the fire. He picked up the sack containing the assault rifles and got to his feet. He was watching the fire as Eureka was stripping down to her bra and panties.

"When you're done burning your clothes, I left the stuff out on the sink for you to use to clean the gunpowder residue from your hands." He told her as he turned to leave with the sack slung over his shoulder.

Eureka nodded, "Where are you going?"

"To stash these until the morning." He held the sack off of his shoulder just a tad bit. "I gotta cat I work with down in China Town that handles them for me. Police will never get their pink hands on them."

He kissed her on the cheek and went off to handle his business. She placed her clothes into the fireplace and glanced over her shoulder, surprised to see Fear descending the staircase down into the basement. A frown equipped her face and she snuck over to the basement's doorway. When she stole a glance down inside she saw him reaching the last step and turning at the left of the staircase. She couldn't help wondering where he was going to stash the guns. She thought he'd hide them in the closet if nowhere else.

Eureka was quiet and careful as she tipped toed down the staircase. She made it about halfway down before easing her head into view so she could see what Fear was doing. She found him knocking on the wall in a certain rhythmic pattern. The wall shot up into the ceiling and he proceeded inside into the darkness. A light came on and she heard some sifting around, a minute the illumination died and he came out. He went pounded on the wall once and the wall shot back down. From there she hurried back up the staircase as quickly and as quietly as she could.

Eureka didn't know what Fear was hiding inside of that secret room of his but she was going to find out one day.

Tranay Adams

CHAPTER SIX

All that could be heard was their heavy breathing as they both were intertwined in the arms of lust. Her micro braids were sprawled on the sheets and her eyes where nothing more than white slits. Her thin red lips were parted and her forehead was beaded with sweat. She clawed at his back with her red acrylic manicured nails drawing a soft growl from his thick lips as his hips moved in a circular motion, hitting that spot that could have her gushing like Old Faithful. The back of his neck as well as his back was shiny from his perspiration. He was digging her out and licking up her throat with his warm, wet tongue. She was a little salty from her sweating but he didn't mind because her pussy was sweet, sweeter than a Hershey's kiss and he couldn't get enough of it. Damn, it was good, so good he threw caution to the wind and slid up in her raw for the first time ever. He was glad he didn't, until now, he didn't know what he had been missing out on.

He licked along her jaw line and stopped at her chin, lightly pulling on her bottom lips. He licked the opening of her lips until they came apart. His tongue seeped in and they began kissing, gently at first then harder. Amidst of their kissing, he lay into her swiftly causing her thick chocolate legs to wrap around the lower half of his back. He brought his head up and looked down into her face as he stroked her, grooving to an imaginary tune.

Her face was turned to the side and her eyes were still to their white. She gasped with each long, deep, thrust her threw into her shaved sex. A crooked grin grew on his face as he watched her enjoy the fruits of his labor. Sweat trickled from his brow and he quickly swiped it away, keeping up the pace of his stroking.

"Look at me." He rasped, breathing hard but not bothering to stop. He was in full control of his mind, functions, and her body. When she didn't do as he said, he repeated himself. "Look at me, baby." This time she looked at him, but her face still bore the same mask of pleasure it always had. "Whose pussy is this?" He sped up his delivery a little. "Huh, baby? Who pussy is this?"

"Yo—yours," she stammered.

"What's my name?"

He asked, slightly choking her about the neck, not enough to hurt her but enough so she could feel his hand there. He sped up two notches more, diving deeper into her slippery pink hole.

"Haa—haa—haa. La—La." Her head tilted back further into the pillow, nearly burying her head into it. Her mouth was stuck open as he slung his dick deeper and deeper inside of her pussy. It took a time before she could gather what wits she could and answer him, "Lavonnnnnnte's!"

"That's right," he said, frowning and biting down on his bottom lip. He squeezed her neck tighter and fucked her deeper and passionately.

"Ah, ssssss, fuck, that's it, that's it…" She whined with her eyes tight and her mouth wide enough to see her uvula.

"I'm 'bout to fucking cum!"

Aww, shit, baby, me too," he said through squared jaws and a face displaying the intensity he was putting out. He squeezed her neck even tighter. He pumped even faster. Her legs locked around his waist. She wanted to keep him there until he got her off. She fell silent and her eyebrows rose and her mouth quivered. The only sounds were his grunting and the headboard bouncing off of the wall.

"Ahhhhh!" She finally came and her legs danced, relinquishing his waist.

"Aww, shit! Sssssss, I'm about to…" Still in motion, he tilted his head back wearing the same mask of pleasure that she once was. His lips trembled as he could feel his balls swelling and all of that rich cream rushing up his dick. "I'm about…"

"Lavonte!" A voice rang from his rear.

"Oh, shit!" Lavonte's head snapped in the direction the voice came. Shock overcame his face when he found Fear and Anton standing in his doorway, both gripping burners. Fear was wearing a not so friendly expression.

"Man, fuck you doing here?" Lavonte rolled off of Johnne, pulling the sheets over his nakedness. She sat up in bed looking scared and pulling the sheet up over her ample breasts. Her eyes shifted back and forth between the killer and his lingering minion. The presence of their bangers told her that they came there for something and if they didn't get what they wanted then shit was going to get real   ugly,   real   fast.

"Relax, Big Dawg, we just came here to talk." He strolled over to the bed and sat down on the edge, body twisted so he'd have the couple in his sight.

"Well, I'll just grab my things and leave. I don't wanna be all in y'all business." Johnne slid her naked ass out of bed and reached for her panties.

"Bitch, you betta get cho ass back in that bed." Anton stepped up with intimidating eyes and his banger at the ready mark. Johnne eased right back into the bed, getting under the sheets.

"I thought so." He posted up against the wall and folded his arms across his chest. He mad dogged homegirl and made her uncomfortable. She couldn't even stand to look in his direction, she was so frightened.

"Wha—wha—what is it that you wanna talk about?" Lavonte stuttered. He knew the killer's resume and he didn't want end up on the wrong side of a bullet.

"Money."

"Mo—mo—money?" He stuttered.

"Yes, mo—mo—money," Fear mocked him. "Let a nigga hold something."

"What if I say I don't got nothing?" He swallowed hard as he tested the waters, a ball of nervousness forming in his stomach.

"Then I'll send some hot shit through that dingy ass doo-rag!" His face tightened at the center and formed a scowl as he pointed his .9mm with the silencer at him. He cracked an evil smile hoping that homeboy would try him so he could open up his face.

Lavonte threw up his arms and leg to guard his face fast as if his limbs would deflect the assassin's bullets if he decided to shoot.

"Alright, man, chill!" he shouted fearfully. "I've gotta couple of grand in my top nightstand drawer, it's yours!"

"That's more like it." Fear lowered his banger at his side. He pulled the nightstand drawer open and moved aside the boxers and wife beaters until he uncovered the money. He motioned Anton over. He came over holding a pillowcase, watching as he threw a thick wad of dead presidents secured by a rubberband into it.

"Damn, G, that's all of my trap," Lavonte complained. "You ain't gon' leave a nigga nothing?"

"If you don't knock it off with that playing broke shit." Fear gritted his teeth. "I know there's plenty more where that came from. Where's the rest of it?"

"You robbing me and we're supposed to be partners."

"Partners," he laughed and tapped Anton. "Yo, you hear this nigga?" Anton screwed up his face and shook his head. "We aren't partners in shit, homeboy! I don't respect dudes like you, you sold yo peoples out for some pussy." He nodded to Johnne. "Where they do that at? They for damn sho' don't do that where I'm from, and that's Trillville! Now where the rest of that paper 'fore I plaster your noodles to that headboard behind you?"

"That's all I got, fam, that's on my dead momma. Michelle, rest in peace." He swiftly crossed his heart in the sign of the crucifix.

Fear gave him the side eye and twisted his lips looking like *Nigga, if you don't get up out of here with that bullshit.*

"Uh huh." He sat his gun on the nightstand and started dumping drawers. He looked to protégé from over his shoulder. "Aye, check ol' girls purse and see what she's holding."

Anton did as he'd been ordered while Fear continued with the dumping of the drawers. All Lavonte and Johnne could do was watch because any other reaction would have had them both in a bad way.

When Fear dumped the third drawer out onto the bed something slightly heavy in black velvet fell out. He smiled fiendishly as he looked up.

Lavonte rolled his eyes and mouthed, "Shiieettt."

"Big homie, she's got half a band." Anton reported after pulling the hundred dollar bills free and throwing the small white purse aside.

"Hold tight to that," he said with his eyes still on Lavonte. "Well, what do we have here? Let's take a peek." He unfolded the velvet and revealed an assortment of jewelry. There was icy white gold rings, gold rings, chains, Presidential Rolex Watches, a Franck Mueller, diamond earrings, etc. All of that shit was shimmering and glistening. Everything looked like something a rapper would wear to the set to shoot the music video to his latest single. Fear folded the velvet back up and dropped it into the pillowcase along with the other goods. He then handed it to his Anton, picked his gun up off of the nightstand and addressed Lavonte. "What else you got, homie?"

Lavonte shook his head fast. "That's it, G, you cleaned me out."

The hit man tightened his jaws. "Don't lie to me, you big head fucka. I should shoot chu in your kneecap."

"On everything I love, man! That's all I got!" He panicked, terrified of getting shot in the kneecap.

"Hoe ass nigga," he shook his head, looking upon him with disgust. "Let's roll," he said to Anton. He turned to leave but something caught his eyes. The enormous aquarium sitting up against the wall. There were sharks and other exotic fish moving through the pretty blue water with a neon light shining in on them. The floor was covered in a bunch of colorful rocks.

Fear narrowed his eyes looking from the aquarium to Lavonte and back again as if he was trying to make heads or tails of something. Abruptly, he pointed his banger at   the   aquarium.

"No, wait, I…" Before Lavonte could finish that

sentence, the killer's gun slightly jumped in his hand as it spat a heat-rock. The aquarium exploded, sending the baby sharks, fish, and water spilling to the floor.

"Are you fucking crazy, man? Do you know how much I paid for that aquarium and those fish?" Lavonte complained until Anton pointed his gun at his bitch-ass, paralyzing his mouth quickly.

"Shut up when a real nigga is conducting business." He sneered like an angry wolf defending its young.

Fear made his way through the drenched floor. He kicked a baby shark aside and picked up two neatly foil packages of cocaine. Tucking his .9mm into the small of his back, he stuck the packages into the pillowcase.

"Oldest trick in the book," he shook his head with twisted lips. "Fuck era you from nigga? The '80's?"

Lavonte smacked the bed with both hands. Frustrated, he ran both of his hands down his face and exhaled. He looked back up at the man that had become the thorn in his side and with pleading eyes, he said, "Come on, my nigga, stall me out. How I'm 'pose to eat with no work? That there is for me to get right." He pointed to the pillowcase that was holding the packages of coke.

"Nigga, save your problems for a shrink 'cause I'm not tryna hear none of that shit." He gave him a hard face. "Fuck what chu going through, pussy. You should have never danced with wolves."

He proceeded toward the door with Anton staying behind with his heater pointed at Lavonte's pitiful ass.

"Fear," he called out his name, looking along the side of Anton. "Come on, man, leave me with something." He begged with his hands together like he was praying.

"We're leaving you with your life, but we could take that too," Anton said.

"Lavonte, baby, just let it go." Johnne tried to touch his arm, but he snatched away.

"Don't touch me, listening to your ass got me tangled and twisted with this goon ass nigga and this bitch." He threw a finger up at Anton, but his eyes were focused on his chick.

"What chu just call me?" The young nigga cut his eyes at him, knowing he couldn't be so stupid as to blatantly disrespect someone that had a gun pointed at him.

"I called you a bitch!" he repeated, eye fucking him. Rocking his head from side to side, he chanted, "Bitch! Bitch! Bitch! Bit— Arghhhhhh!" He shrilled and threw his head back as something hot ripped through his kneecap. He slapped his hands over the spurting hole. Johnne leaned over in bed, trying to tend to him.

Fear turned around grilling Lavonte as Anton trekked passed him. He then winked at Johnne and blew her a kiss before going on about his business.

Fear fenced the jewelry and sold the kilos to a D-Boy he knew from around the way. The money they got for everything wasn't too crazy being they had to split it three ways but it would definitely be enough to pacify them until they handled their situation with The West Coast Connection.

*****

The next day…

The day was pleasantly warm and bright, with the sun shining its good graces on the people below in the cemetery. Bon's funeral brought out his friends, family, and his uncles business associates. Everyone had gathered to pay their respects to the decease and console his loved ones.

Siska stood between Ponytail and Amazon staring at his nephew's coffin as it was lowered into the ground. All he could think about was how he had fucked up by not moving his family out of Los Angeles away from where he operated. If he would have done that, then Bon would still be alive.

"Not, my Bon! Not, my baby! Oh, my God!" Bon's mother sobbed. She tried to jump down into the grave to her son's coffin but a couple of mourners grabbed her before she could. Her eyes were swollen and bloodshot. Her eyes flowed steadily, slicking her cheeks wet. "Please, Lord, take me. Take me instead of him! I beg of you, father. I can't live without my baby!" She went limp in the arms of the men making a hideous face as she hollered.

Damn, Siska closed his eyes and shook his head, hearing his sister perform like she was over the loss of her only child. What he wouldn't give to switch places with the boy just so he wouldn't have to hear her in that state. *I'm sorry kid. If only I could turn back the hands of time and do things differently.*

He felt something manifesting inside of him that he couldn't explain. If he had to guess, it was that something that was conjuring up all kinds of emotions inside of him. Emotions that begged for him to grieve. Emotions that yearned for him to breakdown and cry. As bad as he wanted to bawl and show people how he felt, he refused to. They'd have a better chance seeing 2Pac strutting through downtown Hollywood before they saw tears rolling down his wrinkly cheeks. Any sort of compassion or remorse could be looked at as a sign of weakness. When people looked at him, he wanted them to think of someone powerful and deserving of fear. Someone they knew not to fuck with under any circumstances or they would be squashed like a bug.

"Are you all right, sir?" Ponytail asked in a hushed tone. His eyes never wavered from Bon's mother

"Far from it but listen, I want chu to take out a ransom on Malvo's head. A hundred grand to the man that brings him to me or shows me where he's hiding. I want him alive and well, though. Is that understood?"

"Yes." He nodded, pulling a burnout cell phone from his suit. "I'll get on that right now."

"Thanks, you're a good boy." He rubbed and patted his back. Ponytail went off to make the phone calls he needed to make.

"No mercy," Siska said, watching the mourners trying to get his sister under control as she threw a tantrum. "No mercy when I finally get my hands on you, you bastard." He gritted his teeth and tightened his grasp on his cane.

*****

The double doors of the building swung outward and Constance came strolling in. As soon as she crossed the threshold, she heard the hurried steps of eight pairs of paws and heavy panting heading in her direction. She kneeled down as the twin beasts met her. She massaged their jaws and talked to them like they were babies as they licked her face.

"Heyyy, Evil, how my big man, huh?" She cooed. "How's my big man?"

She turned to Terror and gave him an equal amount of love and affection, allowing him to lick her face.

"Y'all happy to see, Mommy, huh?" Her hands brushed up and down their black shiny coats. "Man's best friend my ass."

"Constance!" Giselle's strained voice rang out from behind the iron door. "Constance is that you? I'm sick, I'm really sick!"

Constance rolled her eyes and rose to her feet, following the sound of the voice as it continued.

"I need—I need some dope bad," Giselle cried. "Real bad. Please, oh, God. Arghhh!" she vomited and something thick and nasty splattered on the floor.

Evil and Terror trotted behind Constance as she took her sweet time walking down the corridor, not giving a damn about the condition that Giselle's dope head ass was in. As far as she was concerned, that was what her ass got for fucking around with drugs in the first place. Sympathy? To hell with sympathy! Sympathy was for AIDS patients and rape victims. And she wasn't either, so fuck her.

"Haa! Haa! Haa!" Giselle breathed heavily. "My fucking stomach...arghhh."

She threw up again just as the iron door was being pulled open. Constance strode in with a Rottweiler on each side of her. The dogs became hostile as soon as they made eye contact with fiend.

Grrrrr! Grrrrr!

"Y'all stop that shit!" Constance spoke to the hounds seriously, looking at each of them. The beasts humbled themselves and sat down on their hind legs.

Constance kneeled down to Giselle, lifting up her chin so she could see her face. It was masked with sweat and she was looking kind of pale. If she didn't know any better, she would have sworn she had the flu, but she was just suffering from withdraw symptoms. Her not having a fix in some time had her stomach twisting in knots.

The femme fatal sat the items Giselle would need to shoot the dope with before her. She then pulled her belt from around her waist and laid it beside everything. Next, she reached inside of her pocket and pulled out three packets of dope labeled Kryptonite, tossing them beside her leg.

Constance stood up. "I'm going to leave you to it, but if you do anything with the shit I left you other than shooting up that poison with it, then my four legged friends here are gonna tear your sickly ass apart, you understand?"

"Yes. Yes, I understand." Giselle nodded rapidly.

"Good. I'll be back once you're done." She walked away leaving the dogs to guard Giselle as she administered her medicine.

Constance didn't mind giving Giselle her own personal key to paradise because she was going to take her through hell shortly. Whether she knew it or not, she was about to participate in leading her own daughter to her death.

CHAPTER SEVEN

Anton and Bootsy sat on the roof of their building staring at the freeway across the way, watching the shiny headlights of the cars traveling back and forth.

"Dad," Anton spoke to his father.

"Yeah, son?" Bootsy responded before taking a sip of his Heineken.

"I wanna be like you when I grow up," he smiled.

"Thanks, baby boy, that means a lot to me." He grinned and gripped his shoulder. "But do me a favor."

"What's that?"

"Don't be like me, be better than me."

"No. I wanna be just like my old man, you're my hero."

Bootsy was about to take another swig of his Heineken but hearing what his boy said stopped him. He allowed the green beer bottle to dangle between his legs and he hung his head, trying to pull himself together. When he looked back up, Anton had a concerned expression across his face. He could tell something was troubling his dad from the glassy look in his eyes. His old man tilted his head back and looked up at the moon, exhaling. It was obvious to him he was drawing back the tears and pain in his heart.

"Are you alright, Dad?" He touched his arm.

Bootsy mustered up a halfhearted smile and casted it at his son, patting him on his hand. "I'm good. But I'm nobody's hero, junior, you hear? I'm struggling, trying to make ends meet and keep food on the table. We're living in Watts, the grandmother of all shitholes. You can't even stand at the goddamn bus stop without wearing a bulletproof vest 'cause if some fool even thinks you're from the wrong projects, he's gonna try to make you cease to exist." He shook his head and took a swig. *"Some hero I am. I couldn't even rescue the people that need me the most—my own family."* He took the time to think to himself before turning to his son. *"Nah, you grow up to be something great, something far better than your old man."*

"Bootsyyyyy!" Giselle called out from below.

Bootsy peered over the edge of the roof., *"Yeah, baby?"*

"Is Ant out there?"

"Yeah, he's up here with me, what's up?"

"Dinner is ready, y'all can come eat."

"Okay." He looked to Anton. *"You heard your momma, gon' and eat, champ. I'll be inside in a minute."*

"Alright." He got to his feet and headed for the ladder. He was about to climb down but then he turned back around to his father. *"Dad."*

Boosty had just taken the bottle from his mouth. He looked to his offspring, raising his eyebrows. *"Huh?"*

"When I grow up, I still wanna be like you. You know why?"

"Why, son?"

"'Cause you're strong and there isn't anything or anyone you're afraid of. You go hard for us. We may not have everything we want, but we have everything we need. You love, protect, provide and sacrifice for us all. That's a man, a man I wanna grow up to be."

"Thank you, son." He cracked a smile, showcasing the gold crown on his side tooth.

"You're welcome, Dad." He continued down the ladder wearing a smile, knowing he'd touched his father.

"Ant! Ant!" Eureka called her baby brother's name.

Anton snapped into the now after hearing his name being called. He blinked his eyes and looked around. All he could see was other surrounding buildings and the rooftops of the ones nearby. He looked at his hands and they were covered in black gloves. He gave himself the once over. He was wearing black fatigues, knee and elbow pads, and equipment for scaling mountains. Slung over his shoulder was a machine gun with a silencer. He looked to Eureka and she was rocking the same attire that he was, machine gun included.

"You good, baby boy? Are you here with me?" she asked, looking into his face and gripping his shoulder.

He slowly nodded as the realization of what they were there for came back to him. The Jackson kids were in downtown Los Angeles on the roof of a fifty foot building. In that very same tenement, on the twentieth floor, was a business owned by The West Coast Connection. Jameson's Notoriety and Republic was a small business that operated as a front for the infamous men. That was one of the places their meetings were held. Often they would switch up locations so that their other meeting spots could be cleaned for bugs.

Anton looked to his sister with determination stitched across his face.

"You sure?" She took him by both shoulders and looked into his eyes.

"I'm ready, let's get it."

"Alright."

They turned around and tugged on the zip lines to make sure they were secure. They then pulled the neoprene masks with the goggles attached to their faces, completely concealing their identities. They gave each other a nod and started down the side of the building, pouncing off of it as they scaled down.

*****

The West Coast Connection sat at the shiny black oak wood table. Bemmy was sitting at the head with a gavel lying beside him. His eyes took a tour of every man rounded out the table. His forehead crinkled noticing there was someone missing. He looked to his left where Honcho was sitting and he shrugged his shoulders.

Bemmy cleared his throat and addressed the men that were present and accounted for. "Has anyone seen Arkane?" They men exchanged glances trying to see if one of them would know of the youngest members' whereabouts. They all looked to the head of their union and shook their heads.

The OG glanced at his watch and saw their mutual associate was about twenty minutes late. Frustrated, he exhaled and talked shit under his breath as he pulled his cell phone from the recess of his suit. Locating Arkane's name, he pressed the automatic dial and placed the cell to his ear. The phone rang four times before it was picked up.

"What's up?"

Bemmy heard Arkane's voice. "Arkane, where the hell are…"

"Hahahaha," he laughed. "Nah, I'm just fucking with chu, I'm busy right now. Probably getting money or up in some pussy or something, you know me. Leave a message at the sound of the beat. Peace."

Bemmy frowned and tightened his jaw, having grown frustrated with Arkane's bullshit. He disconnected the call and tucked the cell phone back inside of his suit.

"Alright, fuck it." He stole everyone's attention, sitting up in his chair. "Youngin' ain't answering, so I take it he's not coming. So, we gone kick this here meeting off without him, agreed?" They all nodded. "Good. Now, as you all know, we have a situation we've yet to address. I'm sure we all know what I'm talking about?" He looked around the table and they all were giving him slight nods.

"You mean dat muddafucka, Fear, right?" Mr. Jun spoke.

"Yeah, him." Bemmy's face balled up, exposing his hatred for the killer.

"You already know where I'm at with it," Honcho began. "I say we pay someone to put one in this puto's head and call it a day, you hear what I'm saying?"

"I for one agree." Mr. Jun conceded. "We all know how he gives it up. He's a living, breathing, killing machine. He could be a real problem for us."

Mike Huggin's snatched the cigar out of his mouth and looked at Mr. Jun. "A problem for us?" He tilted his head back laughing and then brought it back down. "It's just him and what, two or three others that he has under his deodorant? That ain't 'bout shit." He waved his colleagues paranoia off. "I say he's just running his mouth, bluffing at best. He knows he doesn't have enough soldiers and ammo to bump heads with the likes of us."

"If you think Fear was talking outta his ass, then you're sadly mistaken." Bemmy picked up the glass pitcher of ice cold water with slices of lemon floating in it and poured himself a glass. "That man wasn't bluffing. If he said so, then you best believe he has it in his fool ass mind to hunt each and every last one of us down."

"That cock sucka ain't that stupid," Mike claimed. He was looking at Bemmy hoping he would agree but was quickly let down.

"You're right. He's not *that stupid*, he's *that crazy*." He took a sip of water and sat the glass down. "There isn't a goddamn thing in this world that *that* man is afraid of, especially not death. Hell, he welcomes it. Shit, man, do you know how many guys I done sicced this cat on? That son of a bitch is just like one of them wild ass pit bulls with rabies. Once you get 'em started, there ain't no stopping 'em until you put 'em down. And that's exactly what I suggest we do here." He jagged a finger into the table-top.

"Alright, I guess it is better safe than sorry," Mike agreed. He was a little worried now that Bemmy was edgy about the situation with the killer. The OG never seemed this concerned about one man, an entire drug crew maybe, but one mothafucka? Shit, he knew right then that Fear had to be official when it came to that murder shit. Little did he know that homie was in a league all of his own.

"I'm glad you're seeing things my way," Bemmy told him. He then addressed the rest of the bosses at the table. "We need to fly someone out here pronto to clean this stud up 'fore all of our asses are staring up at the fabric inside of a coffin."

"Who do you think we should use?" Mike asked.

"We could use my guys, Capaveli and La' Don," Honcho said. "I vouch for them. They'll make it quick and clean."

"Nah." Mr. Jun shook his head. "We don't need dis ting being traced back to us."

"I agree with Jun here." Bemmy nodded to his Chinese associate. "We don't want that heat."

"How about Cano?" Mike suggested.

"We've used Cano too many times now." Honcho interjected. "Besides, I hear he's locked up anyway."

Bemmy massaged his chin and thought about who they could use to carry out Fear's murder as his associates threw names of certified hitters back and forth. When a name came to mind he ordered the room quiet and just like that all was silent as a grave.

Everyone's attention was focused on the OG. "We'll call in Julian." He took a sip from his glass.

"*Thee* Julian King?" Mike raised an eyebrow.

"How many killahs you know dat go by da name Julian King?" Mr. Jun was annoyed at his question. He and Mike had never gotten along since he found out -he'd been banging his daughter behind his back. The old dude had knocked her up and presented the Jun's with their first golden brown baby. Mr. Jun was fine with doing business with the brothers, but he didn't want any of them in his family tree.

"I'm just tryna make sure, you slanted eyed lil' bastard!" Mike fumed, scrunching up his face and squaring his   jaws.

"You mind your tongue 'fore I snatch it outta ya head, yes?" Mr. Jun's eyebrows arched as he pointed his finger   threateningly.

"If you've got the nerve, then I've got the mind to put one through your thinker." Mike thumbed his nose as he lay back in his chair, pulling his suit open and exposing the pistol in the holster underneath his arm.

"You threatening me, bish?" Mr. Jun's face flushed with redness. He was -angry. He slammed his fist down on the table top and rattled the glasses, sending ripples through the water inside of the pitcher. He was so heated his eyes had turned glassy and bloodshot.

"All that loud talk may frighten your kids but it for damn sure don't move nothing here, homeboy." Mike mad dogged him as he mashed out his cigar in the ashtray, preparing for a confrontation.

Mr. Jun jumped to his feet and Mike was right behind   him.
"Hey! Hey! Hey!" Bemmy raised his voice, looking from Mike to Mr. Jun who were staring each other down. "Knock it off!" The men held one another's glares for a time longer before sitting back down into their respective seats. "We've gotta 'nough to worry about with this fucking vengeful ass hit-man out there plotting to put us in a freezer. We don't need a conflict spilling over into our own house."

"We'll settle this later, tough guy." Mike made his hand into the shape of a gun and pointed it at the Chinese drug lord as he went to sit down in his chair.

"When da next song comes on, we'll most definitely dance." Mr. Jun assured him with a cocky smile before sitting back down.

Bemmy picked up the gavel from the table. "Do we all agree to have Julian King handle this disgruntled ex-employee of ours?"

They all nodded and he slammed the gavel down, adjourning The West Coast Connection's meeting. They grabbed their hats and overcoats. Putting on his hat and then his coat, Bemmy noticed something outside of the floor to ceiling window. His eyes lit up and his mouth snapped open as he screamed with veins forming in his neck, "Get down!" He dove to the floor with everyone following suit, all except Mr. Jun and Mike who moved just a second too slow.

Choot! Choot! Choot! Choot! Choot! Choot! Choot! Choot!

Eureka and Anton dangled outside of the window sweeping their machine guns back and forth across the room. The glass fell like water from a waterfall, sliding across the flat carpeted floor. The bullets looked like lasers shooting through the meeting room, striking chairs and knocking splinters out of the oak wood table, turning it into confetti.

The top of Mr. Jun's head splattered, sending what look like spaghetti sauce everywhere. Next was his chest bursting open as embers ripped through it. Even after he was dead, bullets continued to tatter his suit, shredding the fabric and riddling it with holes. When he hit the floor he was nothing more than a bloody mess dressed up in an expensive suit. Mike was right behind him with half of his dome missing and a chest littered with holes. The horror he experienced before his life was snatched was smeared across his face.

The racket drew the attention of the bodyguards. The door swung open and in first were Honcho's men, Capaveli and La'Don totting guns, followed by the guards of the other bosses. Capaveli and La'Don dove to the floor and left the others to take the heat. The men dropped their guns and danced on their feet, sprinkling blood as their bodies jerked violently from left to right. Their eyes were wide and their mouths were open when their riddled forms hit the floor. Capaveli and La'Don crawled toward the table on their hands and knees hastily. Once they reached the other men, they tucked their heads and guarded them with their arms, wincing. The rapid flow of gunfire continued.

Choot! Choot! Choot! Choot! Choot! Choot! Choot! Choot! Choot! Choot!

Eureka and Anton's machine guns clicked empty and expelled smoke. They released the spent cartridges and reloaded, cocking one into the chambers of the weapons. Hearing police car sirens, they slung them around their backs and scaled down the side of the building as fast as they could.

After a while the bosses slowly began to stir, coming out from their hiding places underneath the table. They cautiously looked around before getting upon their feet.

"Is everyone alright?" Bemmy asked, looking around at everyone.

"I'm straight." Honcho announced, shifting glass from off his clothes. He looked to Capaveli and La'Don. "Are y'all okay, man?"

They nodded, "Yeah, we're good."

"Jun, Mike, how about y'all?" Bemmy looked around but didn't see the Chinaman or Mike. "Jun? Mike?"

"Damn." Honcho eyes casted down at the floor. Everyone moved in to see what he was talking about. Once they reached him they saw Mr. Jun lying on his back with the top of his head missing. The excruciation he experienced was etched upon his face and the hole in his chest was so big you could see the bloody bones that made up his ribcage. Lying right beside him was Mike with pieces of his brain and blood oozing out of the side of his skull. All of the men present crossed their chests in the sign of the crucifix.

Bemmy looked over by the door and saw the dead bodyguards that had the misfortune of getting caught up in the crossfire. Seeing all of the dead bodies enraged him. He stormed off to the opposite side of the room, throwing over a chair.

"You mothafuckaz! Youuu Mothafuckazzz!" He shouted and swung on the air, his eyes consumed by rage. His nostrils flared and his shoulders rose and fell with each breath he took. He was furious.

*****

As Eureka and Anton made it to the ground, a police car was pulling up. Its door swung open just as they unsheathed their bowie knives and sliced the zip lines from their person.

"Freeze!" The cops shouted in unison.

"Go, I'll cover you!" Anton hollered to his sister. She took off and he whipped around, taking a hold of his machine gun. He pointed it just as the cops were reaching for the tools on their waist. Before they could clear the weapon from their holsters, he was already pulling the trigger…

Choot! Choot! Choot! Choot! Choot! Choot! Choot! Ping! Ting! Clink! Zing! Kinkkk!

Anton gripped the machine gun firmly as it rattled in his hands, chewing up the police car and leaving behind what looked like a million holes. After he got off, he took off running as fast as he could. When he bent the corner at the end of the building, he saw Eureka waiting on him with her machine gun pointed. If the cops came around that corner and not her brother, she was going to turn them into a statistic. The Jackson kids ran side by side, occasionally looking over their shoulders. Their adrenaline was pumping, their hearts were racing, and they were moving like a couple of runaway slaves with hounds on their heels.

"Shit!" Eureka looked ahead and saw a police car approaching.

"These mothafuckaz are on us!" Anton spotted the cops he'd bust at on at his rear.

"Hit the alley, I gotcho back!" Eureka shouted to her brother.

Anton followed his sister's orders. Once he was clear, she hoisted up her machine gun and pulled the trigger, sweeping it across. Sparks flew from off the light post, the side of the building and the sidewalk. One cop dove in front of a parked Scion while the other dove behind a building. She wasn't trying to hit them she was just trying to keep them off her and baby brother's ass.

Eureka high tailed it up the sidewalk. Stopping at the mouth of the alley, she aimed at the oncoming police car and sprayed it. Hot shit flew through the windshield and shattered the glass, while the rest tatted up the hood of the vehicle. The police car swung around in the middle of the street. The doors flew open and two cops hopped out with their guns at the ready. They joined up with the other two cops and together they moved in on the alley. When they swung out into the alley with their weapons pointed they found a lady in a business suit lying on her back. The contents of her purse lay beside her as she bawled on the ground, holding her bleeding nose.

"They went that way!" Eureka sounded muffled with her hand over her nose as she pointed down the alley.

Boc! Boc! Boc! Boc!

The sound of successive gunfire drew the cops like bees to honey and they took off down the alley. Eureka got up from the ground touching her bloody nose and looking to her hand as she approached the trash bin. She threw open the lid of the dumpster and grabbed Anton by his hand, pulling him up out of the nasty container. He landed on his feet and fixed his baseball cap. He was dressed in a little league baseball uniform and wearing a catcher's mitt.

"Come on." Eureka struck up the opposite path of the alley with Anton following closely beside her. They could hear the police helicopter approaching from above. They ran down the alley with the big fluorescent light following closely behind. Just as the light was going to shine on them, they ducked off behind another trash- bin. They huffed and puffed out of breath as Eureka debated their next move.

*****

"Shit!" Fear cursed under his breath after being told to move by a cop because he was parked in a red-zone. The hit man was disguised as an Indian man rocking a turban and a red dot at the center of his forehead. His eyebrows and mustache were also bushy to give him the appearance of an older man. He circled around the block twice hoping someone would be leaving so he could get their parking space. When he couldn't find one on the side he was supposed to be waiting, he parked on the opposite side of the building near the alley.

He threw the taxi in neutral, keeping the car running. He drummed his fingers on the steering wheel and took in his surroundings as he awaited his comrade's arrival.

Hearing police sirens approaching, he leaned toward the windshield and peered ahead. A police car jumped the curb of the tenement Eureka and Anton had planned the assault on. As soon as the cops hopped out, they were met with rapid gunfire, causing them to dive to the ground and take cover. The chattering of the weapon made people scatter and scramble, trying to get out of the way before they caught something hot.

Fear looked down the alley were he figured Eureka and Anton would pass if they were running. Shortly, he saw them run into the alley and strip down to the second set of clothes they had on. Anton crawled inside of the dumpster while Eureka punched herself in the mouth, busting it and falling to the ground. Four cops rushed the alley with their guns drawn, advancing on Eureka. Feeling he needed to act fast,

Fear withdrew his .9mm from the glove-box and

screwed off the silencer. He pulled out of his parking space and as he was driving off, he pointed his banger into the air. *Boc! Boc! Boc! Boc!*

*****

Eureka placed the Booth-Tooth headset on her ear and withdrew her cell phone, placing a call. The line rang but no one answered.

"Fuck!" She cursed, frustratedly.

"What? What happened?" Anton became concerned.

"He's not answering."

"You think they got 'em?"

"I don't know, but we've gotta get outta here." Eureka looked up and down the alley, trying to think where they should run next.

"This place is gonna be crawling with The Ones in a minute if they haven't already arrived."

Anton nodded in agreement.

Eureka tapped Anton and faced the direction they were going to run to. "Come on." She moved to run but two police cars slid to a halt blocking off the alley. They both wore spooked expressions. Eureka drew her Glock from out of her purse and threw it aside, while Anton pulled a .22 from his sock. They'd be damned if they spent the rest of their young lives behind a barbwire fence. They'd go out in a blaze of gun smoke and blood before they'd face prosecution.

"Drop it!" A voice rang at their rear. They didn't even have to look. They knew that it was the cops.

Eureka and Anton took deep breaths and dropped their weapons. When they did this, the cops from the opposite end of the alley hopped out of their cars drawing steel. The siblings did like they were ordered, putting up their hands and getting down on their knees, hands behind their   heads.

They heard two pair of booted feet moving in their direction from the back which meant there were two badges approaching them. Staring ahead, they saw the other Donut Lovers hopping back inside of their vehicles so they could drive down the alley where they were.

"Damn," Eureka said, closing her eyes.

"It was all good just a week ago." Anton quoted Jay-Z lyrics with a hard face. Whatever his punishment would be, he was ready to take it.

The brother and sister heard static, some numbers being spat and then the cop's voice as he spoke into the small radio transceiver on his shoulder.

"I've got the sus..."

Vrooooooooooom!

The sound of bodies being struck by a car, tumbling upon it and falling down to the ground came from their rear. They then heard a sharp whistle. They looked over their shoulders and saw Fear in a yellow taxi cab, waving them over. The cops lay sprawled on the ground moaning in agony. Eureka and Anton snatched up their guns and dipped   inside   of   the   taxi.

Fear hopped out of the taxi just as the brother and sister approached. He wore a surgical mask over his nose and mouth. In his hands were three flash grenades. He pulled the pins out of each one and launched them in the oncoming police cars direction. The grenades hit the ground and skidded, exploding with a deafening sound and blinding light. Fear ducked back inside of the taxi and came back up with an MM1 grenade launcher. Gripping the weapon tightly and pointing it down the alley, he pulled the trigger multiple times. The drum on the launcher twisted as it spat smoke grenades rapidly. He didn't stop firing until the grenade launcher was spent and smoke was screening the alley. Afterwards, he pulled the mask down on his neck, tossed the weapon into the front passenger seat and peeled off.

"Y'all all right? Ya'll good?" Fear stole a look at them through the rearview mirror.

"Yeah." Eureka nodded, breathing hard. "Ant, you okay?"

"I'm straight." He responded, out of breath.

"Oh, fuck!" Fear cursed, seeing something he didn't want to see.

"What?" Eureka's eyebrows rose. His response was nodded toward the windshield. Coming their way was a fleet of police car with their sirens blaring.

"Y'all play it cool, act natural." He focused bore an emotionless face.

Surprisingly, the fleet of black and white car zoomed right past them. Everyone relaxed a little having made it past them without getting stopped.

"Home free," Anton concluded. As they passed the building he and Eureka had sprayed the floor that The West Coast Connection was having a meeting in, he turned and looked out of the back window along with Eureka. Police cars, the coroners van, and an ambulance were parked out front. The West Coast Connection were either standing around or refusing to answer the cops' questions. Bemmy and Honcho were standing over Mr. Jun and Mike's bodies as sheets were draped over them. As if they could feel someone watching them, they looked directly at the back window of the taxi at Anton and Eureka's faces. The OG's faces twisted with anger and they clenched their teeth, causing their jaws to pulsate. It was then that they realized the two kids riding in the back of the taxi were down with Fear, they could feel it in their guts.

*****

"Y'all didn't drop any of the old heads?" Fear looked from Eureka to Anton with his hands planted down on   the   tabletop.

"Two of 'em," Anton said from where he was licking a Swisher closed. "Jun and Mike."

Fear nodded feeling good that they'd taken out two of The West Coast Connection's members. He wanted to get the whole lot with that move they made, but any day one of theirs was below ground was a good day.

"That's it?"

"We took out a few of their bodyguards but that's it." Eureka loaded up the slugs in the weapons they would use in the next hit. "The rest of them niggaz got the fuck up outta the way when we started popping off."

"We should have just jumped down in that room and touched all of them old niggaz, straight up." Anton's eyes were focused on the Swisher as he swept the flame of a lighter back and forth underneath.

"Nah," Fear shook his head. "Y'all did right. It was too risky getting at them niggaz downtown anyway. One-Time stay rolling back and forth through there."

"Who's next up?" Anton asked, blowing smoke into air.

Fear's response was closing his eyes and picking the bowie knife up from off of the table. He flipped it over in his palm and turned to the wall. There were pictures of The West Coast Connection's members as well as their bodyguards. The ones that had been eliminated had a red X drawn over their faces. Fear pounced the knife in his hand before lifting it, throwing it like a pitcher would a baseball. The knife spun around in circles, looking like a white blur en route to its target.

Whock!

The blade buried halfway inside of the photo of the man that would be their next target. Eureka and Anton came to stand beside him. He peeled his eyelids open and folded his arms across his chest.

It's time to pay for your sins, Fear thought, narrowing his eyes as he took a pull from the blunt Anton had passed him.

Someone had just ended up on the wrong side of his gun.

CHAPTER EIGHT
The next night…

Melissa walked down the hall of her complex leaning to one side as she toted the baby seat her child was in. Nearing her condo's door, she fished inside of her purse for her keys. Finding them, she opened the door and pushed her way inside.

When she flipped on the light switch, she could have shit her panties when she saw two masked man and woman sitting on her couch. They were both dressed in all black and carrying some shit the natives in Iraq would bust with. Their eyes were glassy and threatening as if they wish she would try some shit just so they'd have an excuse to leave her lying face down in a pool of her own blood. As bad as she wanted to run back out of the door she didn't. She was toting her baby boy and was sure she would be slowed down by him. That would be all of the time the intruders needed to pull the trigger of those machine guns and do her up something nasty.

"If you're thinking about running, let me be the first to tell you that it's so notta good idea." Fear warned her. "All that's gon' do is make me mad and send this baby at cha." He switched hands with the machine gun. "Do me a favor sweetheart, close that door behind you and step inside." She went to move a little too fast and the next thing he said startled her because his voice slightly rose. "Move!" His voice boomed. "Very slowly." She did as he said at the pace he'd demanded.

"Have a seat." He threw his head toward the spot on the couch beside him. She hesitantly walked forward.

"Move yo' ass!" Eureka gritted and kicked her in the ass. She stumbled forward and fell on the carpet, burning   her   knees.

"Come on. Get up." She grabbed the woman up under her arm and pulled her up roughly, shoving her over on the couch. She fell awkwardly and her hair bounced. Tears were in her eyes and she looked from the masked intruders terrified. Her eyes settled on her baby and she panicked. She went to move to grab the baby seat and Eureka pointed her machine gun at her.

"Ahhh!" She quickly cupped her hands to her face and hot tears splashed from her moist eyes. She trembled hard as if her bones were chattering.

"I done told you before to slow your roll." Fear told her. "My partner over there is trigger happy. That toy I gave her is brand new and she's dying to put a body on it. I just pray to God is not yours 'cause I'd hate to see that happen." He shook his head like it would be such a shame. "Now what's your name?"

"Melissa." She sobbed, wiping tears from her eyes.

"Alright, Melissa, I'm gonna ask you a yes or no question. And I want a yes or no answer. Do you understand?" She nodded rapidly. "Good. Do you want to live?" He looked her dead in her eyes and her heart skipped a beat. She was scared, real scared. She could feel her bladder filling as she stared into his dark soulless eyes. She knew without a doubt he'd leave her inside of her condo face   down.

"Ye—yes." Melissa nodded.

"Great. Answer this question and we'll leave you here unharmed. Ready?"

"Yes."

"Where can we find Honcho?"

"I don't know. I swear to God I don't know." She sobbed hard, fearful of what the masked men and woman would do if she didn't give them the answer they wanted.

"This bitch lying!" Eureka called it how she saw it.

"Relax," Fear raised a hand. "See, here's where the problem comes in Melissa…" he leaned in closer with a pair of menacing eyes "…I don't believe you." He whispered, causing her heart to smack up against her chest plate. "Melissa the last thing I'd hate to do is leave you here with your thoughts splattered all over this here pretty chin chiller carpet." He looked around at the thick beige carpet. "Hear me when I say I'm not tryna take it there, boo." He spoke soothing and calmingly. "All I want to know is the whereabouts of your sponsor. You give me that and all of this will seem like a bad dream, we'll be gone, my right hand to God." He lifted a hand and swore with an expression as serious as cancer.

Melissa was one of the five younger women Honcho took care of. She and one of the other girls bore his children, which made her one of the upmost importance in his life. He took them out of the slums and moved them out to nice cozy tenements out in Beverly Hills. He made sure their condos' rent were paid, the car note was taken care of, they had food in the house and he gave them a generous allowance every week. It was safe to say Melissa was a kept woman. She would never have to lift a finger for as long as she lived. All she had to do what take care of their baby boy, CJ, Carlos Jr.

For as good as life had been since she'd gotten herself knocked up by the Mexican drug lord, right now she was regretting the day she'd ever laid eyes on him. She loved the attention she got being one of the women of

Carlos Radames. His status opened a lot of doors for her and she was the benefactor of many spoils but now she couldn't care less about any of that. Why? Because wasn't none of that shit going to save her life.

Melissa stared dead into Fear's eyes and knew without a doubt he would leave her sleeping forever. Even so, she couldn't give up Honcho. She loved him far too much. She'd much rather sacrifice her own life for his.

"I'm sorry." She slapped her hand over her mouth as she shook her head rapidly, tears raining from her eyes causing her eyeliner to run. She closed her eyes and hoped her murder would be a quick and painless one.

"Waaaaa! Waaaaa! Waaaaa!" The baby wailed, stealing everyone's attention.

Fear looked over to the baby then peeked back at Melissa, smiling evilly. "Watch her." He ordered Eureka, slinging the strap of the machine gun over his shoulder as he headed over to the baby. Melissa panicked, looking back and forth between the killer and the baby seat.

Once she saw he was headed for her baby, she motioned toward them shouting, "Noooo." But she jumped back when Eureka turned his machine gun on her.

"Move again and that's yo' ass." she warned.

All Melissa could do was stand there and watch as Fear scooped the baby out of the baby seat. He rocked the little guy in his arms and looked upon him, making faces. The little fella smiled and made cute noises as he tickled his   chin.

"Lil' nigga is cute. You sure he's Honcho's son?"

"Yes." She nodded, tears falling rapidly. She wiped them from under each eye as they fell.

The killer pushed the oven to the center of the kitchen floor so Melissa could see it in full view. He yanked open the door and inserted the baby inside. Seeing this, made her look alive, especially once she saw him close the door back. He turned the dial to boil and took a step back with a wicked smirk plastered on his face.

"Noooooooo!" She jumped to her feet and shoved Eureka aside. She dashed over to the oven, but Eureka tripped her up. She fell hard on her stomach, grimacing as the wind was knocked out of her. She then grabbed her up under her arm and threw her narrow ass on the couch.

He pointed the machine gun in her face and barked, "Try that again," he warned. "On my momma, I'ma pump you fulla some hot shit. You understand me?"

She nodded her head and sniffled. She looked to Fear and he was pulling the sleeve of his black sweatshirt up uncovering his digital watch. He glanced at the time then looked up at her, resting his arm on the top of the oven.

"Alright I figure you've gotta 'bout three minutes before lil' Honcho there starts cooking. So I suggest you tell me what I wanna know. Not now, but right now."

"You monster, he's just a baby!"

"You think I care? Fuck this lil' mothafucka," he kicked the oven's door. "He didn't come from me. You wanna save 'em yo ass betta start moving them dick suckers." A while of silence passed and he glanced at his

114

watch again. "One and a half minute left." He announced then looked through the square glass window of the oven, Honcho's offspring was wailing. He turned back around to the baby's mother. "Yeah, he's starting to sweat in there."

Melissa dropped to her hands and knees slobbering and sobbing as she hung her head, tears dripping into the thick carpet and staining her hands.

"One minute." The hit man told her.

"Okay! Alright!" She threw her head up crying, shoulders shuddering. "You win. I'll tell you."

"You betta catch diarrhea at the mouth 'cause you've gotta 'bout half a minute 'fore this lil' nigga comes outta that there oven scorched."

Melissa vomited the location of Honcho's mansion out in the Suburbs of Los Angeles. When she was done, she pleaded for the assassin to give her *her* baby back. Fear took his time opening the oven and recovering CJ. Receiving her son, the mother checked him thoroughly. A smile curled her lips seeing her bundle of joy was okay.

"Cut the phone lines and retrieve her cell phone," Fear ordered Eureka. With the flick of her wrist, she brandished a shiny blade and did as her mentor commanded. She then dumped the contents of Melissa's purse out on the floor and rummaged through it with her foot until she uncovered her cell. She picked it up and broke it in half, letting the halves drop to her feet.

"I trust after we leave you aren't going to contact Honcho or the police, right?" Fear looked at her like *Bitch if you say anything other than no, I'ma dead your ass right here.*

"No." She shook her head, wiping her wet face with

her sleeve. "I won't tell him nothing. I won't say a thing. I swear on my son's life."

"Great answer," he replied, looking her dead in the eyes and meaning everything he said next. "I'd sure hate to find out you opened your mouth 'cause that would guarantee lil' man would become an orphan. We wouldn't want that, now would we?" She shook her head *no*.

He threw the power cord at her feet. She looked up and a frown corrupted her face, it was a part to the oven, a part that it couldn't work without.

"The monster has a heart." He told her before waving Eureka on and making his exit.

*****

The night was quiet, still, and cold. So cold he could see his breath every time he breathed. His fists were wrapped up in bandages and he was naked from the neck down, clad in only black parachute pants. His neck was on a swivel as it took in all of the 2 x 4's surrounding him. They were planted firmly inside of the ground and were wrapped in thick layers of torn sheet. His fists came before his eyes as he slid his legs apart, positioning himself in a fighter's stance. He closed his eyes for a moment and was transported to that faithful night. Not the night he and his sister were forced to go on the run from the tyrant known as Malvo, but the night his father was taken away from him.

Bloc! Bloc!

The rush of gunshots echoed throughout Anton's mental. He could literally hear his father screaming as his flesh was scorched by the sizzling bullets. Over and over again the images of Bootsy being murdered and stripped of his valuables would play within the theater of his imagination. It was a trip to him because he wasn't there when it had happened. And even though he knew he'd only been shot once, his mind tortured him with the thoughts of his father being brutally murdered.

Crack! Thwack! Wrack!

The 2 x 4's made their own music when his fists and feet struck them. His body was glistening with perspiration. He was lost within the depths of his thoughts and was attacking the faceless killer that had murdered his father. He could hear the murderer's cries as he met with his   lightening   quick   assault.

"Stop, please!"

"Ooof!"

"Fuck a please! You killed my dad, you bastard!"

The youngster growled, lashing out like a wolverine. He attacked the boards viciously causing them to make even louder noises. He was breathing hard and his form was running with sweat like as if it was beads of water from a shower. You couldn't tell him he wasn't face to face with the son of bitch that had stolen his old man's life. He could see him grimacing and doubling over as he tore into him. He witnessed his head whip around after a solid right to the jaw, a spray of blood going through the air. Finally, the murderer dropped to his knees. Anton followed up with a haymaker. He drew all of his strength into his fist and fired on the 2 x 4. *Waammp!* The board broke, its top half flipping through the air. It came down and stabbed into the lawn.

Anton dropped down to his hands and knees, his head bobbing as he panted, dripping sweat.

Unbeknownst to Anton, Fear and Eureka had arrived home not long ago and were watching him from the kitchen window.

"I got 'em, I got 'em, Dad," he spoke to his father. "I beat 'em, I beat 'em for you." He staggered to his feet and approached Bootsy who was standing before him with open arms. It wasn't him though. It was actually one of the 2 x 4's. The youngster was missing his pop's so much he'd become delusional.

"You did good son, real good." He imagined Bootsy's voice. *"Come here. Give your old man a hug."*

"I missed you, Dad. I missed you so much." Anton's emotions got the best of him. Tears manifested in his eyes and took a tour down his cheeks as he moved forth.

"I missed you too, champ. Bring it in." Anton envisioned Bootsy motioning him over with waves of his hands. He bore a smiling face and his entire body was lit as if he was glowing from the inside.

A smirk snaked its way across Anton's lips as he fell into his father's imaginary arms, holding him tightly. He snuggled his face against his chest and cried his heart out. "I know you told me to always be strong, but—but I'm hurting, Dad. I'm hurting so, so much." He sniffled and licked his lips. "It's not easy being—being strong. It's been so hard since you haven't been here."
"It's okay, I'm back now." He kissed him on top of the head, and rubbed his back. Anton hadn't noticed but it wasn't his father who he'd wrapped his arms around. It was

Fear. His eyes were glassy and he could feel the young boy's pain. He wished he could zap all of that hurt that was inside of him so he wouldn't have to feel it, but he knew that was impossible. He would have to deal with his hurt the best way that he knew how.

20 minutes later...

"I say we hit Honcho's monkey ass tonight." Anton slammed his fist into his palm and closed his fingers around it. He was bare chest with a white towel around his neck.

"We can't hit'em tonight without a plan, family." Fear massaged his chin as he was thinking. "He'll most definitely be waiting on us. I'm sure word has spread like the Ebola virus about Arkane's death by now. Them old heads done took extra precautions."

"He's right, Ant." Eureka added her two cents. "After taking out Arkane, Jun, and Mike, Honcho's antennas are definitely going to be up. He's gonna expect us to come gunning for him."

"I hear what chu saying, but I'm telling y'all if we strike tonight they won't be expecting us." Anton assured with his palms down on the table, looking from his sister to his mentor. "Hit these mothafuckaz hard, I mean real hard. They won't know what hit 'em and by the time they do we would have been done executed Honcho's ass and got outta the way."

"We need a plan, junior," Fear eye fucked him and said with a low growl. "We can't go storming in on his soil halfcocked. I'm not doing it. I'm not putting all of our lives at risk."

"Man, this is some bullshit!" Anton threw his towel to the floor. "Fuck the waiting, the time is now! If we keep sitting around, they're gonna eventually find us and dead us! You said these dudes gotta 'nough juice and bread to put a small country to sleep, right? Well, what do you think they can do to the three of us?" He stopped and waited for Fear's response.

The killer settled down in his chair and cleared his throat before saying another word.

"I gave my order and my word is final." Fear shot him a stern expression. From the look on his face, it was understood he wasn't bullshitting, and any more lip from the youngling could possibly lead to him getting his ass kicked.

Things were quiet for a time with Eureka looking back and forth between her brother and her man. Then finally one of them spoke and broke the silence, "Alright," Anton picked up the towel. "It's your call."

He slung the towel over his shoulder and moved for the hall. He only stopped when he was called back.

"You know the penalty for disobedience?" He gave him a look like *Fuck up and I won't hesitate to tax that ass.*

"Like the back of my hand." He held up his hand which had L.O.E inked on it. Those were his parting words before he vanished into the mouth of the hallway.

"Baby brother's gotta head harder than titanium." Fear gave Eureka his acknowledgement.

"Yeah, Ant's as stubborn as they come, I can't argue with that."

"You think he'll go after Honcho?"

Eureka looked from Fear to the hallway then back. "I wouldn't put it passed him."

Fear hopped up from his chair and motioned for Eureka to follow him.

*****

Anton stormed into his bedroom and slammed the door behind him. He threw himself on the bed and clasped his hands behind his head, staring up at the ceiling.

"Why don't they ever listen to me? It's 'cause they look at me as a kid, I bet. Probably think I don't know what I'm talking about. All of my life, niggaz been shutting me out 'cause I was too little or too young. I hate that shit, man! Grrrr," he turned on his side and punched the bed, heatedly.

"What happened, Champ?" Bootsy turned Anton's chin from left to right as he inspected his face.

"He got into a fight with Tyrone." Eureka informed him.

"That grown ass man up the street? Nigga got me fucked up," Bootsy's brows furrowed. "Let me get my shit." He moved to go into the closet to get the .44 Magnum revolver he had stashed inside of a tin box.

"Nah, Daddy, Tyrone ain't but two years older than Ant."

Bootsy looked surprised. His mouth was stuck open. "That big swollen mothafucka look like he at least thirty. What're they feeding these kids these days?"

"Beats me," Eureka shrugged.

"Reka, gon' get me the First-Aid kit outta the bathroom cabinet."

Once Eureka was gone, he tended to his son, giving his cuts and bruises a thorough exam.

"That one there is a beaut," he said of his swollen, blackened eye. "You use the shit I taught you?"

"Yeah, I got 'em good, Daddy," Anton smiled weakly. "But he was too big. He got the best of me. I'm too light to fight and too thin to win." He hung his head shamefully, having been given a hard time for being one of the smallest kids that attended his school.

"That's bullshit!" Bootsy spat, peevishly. "Long as there's breath in your lungs and you got these," he held up his clenched fists. "You've always gotta chance to win. I don't give a shit if a son of a bitch is seven feet tall and you're three foot nothing, your chance at winning a brawl is just as good as his. Is all about the size of the fight in ya son."

"But Daddy I can't..."

"Fuck you just say to me?" Bootsy cut his eyes at his son. He looked like he was about to smack sparks out of him. Anton hung his head. "You look a man in his eyes when he's addressing you, I taught you better than that." Anton lifted his head up, locking eyes with his old man. "Can't is for losers. If you got can't up here," he tapped his temple with his finger, "then you've already lost before you've even begun. 'I can't' shouldn't roll off of any man's tongue. If it does, he's not fit to call himself a man. He's nothing more than a male. That's it." He scooted his chair closer and took his boy by the hands, keeping eye contact. "I will and I can is all you know, son. When there is a will there is a way. Your dedication, your determination, your drive to succeed and achieve is enough to conquer anything life puts in your way. You hear me?"

"Yes, sir."

"*Come on, junior.*" *He smiled, playfully punching the boy.* "*You sounding like a lil' old bitch right now, put some bass in your voice.*"

"*Yes, sir!*" *he spoke loud and clear, smiling.*

"*Alright now.*"

"*Alright then.*"

Eureka returned with the First-Aid kit and handed it to her father. "*Here you go, Daddy.*"

"*Thank you, baby.*" *He took the kit and sat it on the table. He then grabbed two cold ones out of the refrigerator and began cracking open their caps.* "*Baby girl, your momma up in there?*"

"*Nope, fast asleep.*" *She smiled, knowing what he had in mind.*

"*Good. We can celebrate then.*"

Eureka and Anton exchanged confused glances.

"*Celebrate what? That I got my ass whopped?*" *Anton spoke up, garnering a look from his father about his foul mouth.* "*I mean I got my butt whopped.*"

Bootsy passed his children a beer each before picking his own back up.

"*You're gonna whop fat Tyrone's ass tomorrow.*" *He predicted the future.* "*And after you do, we're all going out to celebrate.*"

The next day Anton, with the coaching of his father, beat the brakes off of Tyrone. He left the kid on the asphalt with a bloody mouth and missing teeth. He was snoring hard and loud. Bootsy left the block $200 dollars richer due to his betting on his son whipping the bully's ass. He gave Eureka and Anton fifty bucks a piece, and they went out for root beer floats, which was Anton's favorite.

"I can take 'em, I can take 'em alone." Anton sat up in bed after reminiscing, planting his feet onto the carpet. "Yeahhh." He slammed his fist into his palm and jumped up from off of the bed. He strapped on a Kevlar bulletproof vest, slipped on a black thermal and combat boots. After donning gloves, he strapped on a bowie knife, two chrome thangs and a sleek black motorcycle helmet. Fully equipped, he turned the doorknob but it wouldn't budge. He frowned as he twisted and turned the knob trying to get it to open. Once he figured he'd been locked in, he started kicking it with all of his might. It wouldn't give, though.

"Goodnight, don't let the bed bugs bite," Fear said from the other end.

"Open the door, goddamn it!" Anton shot back.

"Notta chance, take that ass to sleep," he responded. "We'll talk about how we're gonna deal with ol' Honcho in the AM."

"Reka!" Anton hollered, trying to reason with his sister

"You heard 'em, baby boy. Good night."

"Grrrr."

Woomp!

He punched the door and darted over to the window. He tried to turn the latch so he could open it but the goddamn thing wouldn't budge.

"Fuck!" he shouted, he turned back around to the door. A light bulb came on inside of his head and he snatched one of the pearl handle chrome thangs free from its holster. A mischievous smile enveloped his adolescent face as he stormed to the door. He sat his helmet down on the floor and lifted the silenced pistol. A few hushed, well placed bullets made the lock drop to the surface. Anton pushed the door open easily. When he knocked the chair over that was barricading the door, he looked up and down the hallway hoping no one had heard it fall. Sensing the coast was clear, he entered the living room grabbing a mase from off of the wall as he went along. Inside of the garage, he slipped on his helmet and revved up the motorcycle. And just like that, he was gone.

Tranay Adams

CHAPTER NINE

Since Fear had hit the building in downtown Los Angeles, taking out Jun and Mike, Honcho pretty much been staying off of the radar. The only time he left the grounds of his estate was to conduct business or visit one of his many children. Other than that he was at home chilling, trying to figure out the next endeavor that would make his already fat pockets fatter. If his mind wasn't on his business, then it was on the steps to take to rid himself of Fear. The hit man's presence had become like a fly, always swarming around and annoying the hell out him. He thought the highly recommended assassin, Julian King, would be able to relieve him of his stress but he'd gotten word he had problems getting past customs on the account of his record. He had suggested to Bemmy to use another guy, but he insisted on Julian because he believed he was Fear's equal. In the meantime, all he could do was wait to get the word that The Chosen One had touched down on California soil.

Honcho sat inside his study hunched over a box of lemon pepper chicken wings and fries. He sunk his teeth into the wing of the fried bird and pulled back, tearing the meat from its bone like a carnivore.

"Y'all don't won't nothing to eat?" Honcho asked Cappaveli and La'Don. They shook their heads *no*. The young wolves went wherever their boss went. They were his own personal security. Though they didn't speak much, violence was their strong point. They had enough bodies between them to open up their own morgue. "Suit yourself, you missing out, though. This chicken is good as a mothafucka." He was about to tend back to his box of wings when he saw one of his armed guards walk Jynx into his study.

Honcho motioned to the empty chair beyond his desk. Taking his cue, the short stubby man pulled out the chair and planted himself in the seat. He tossed the Crown Royal bag at the center of the table and he snatched it up. He pulled the Crown Royal bag open and pulled out a pretty green bud sprinkled with purple crystals. He brought the bud to his nose, closed his eyes and inhaled its scent. Its enchanting aroma brought a smile to his face. He dropped the bud back on the desk and pulled open his desk drawer. He removed a razor-blade, a pack of Cigallaros, and a Zippo-lighter. With what he needed to fix his blunt on the desk top, he dumped the rest of the contents out and went about the task of breaking it down.

Honcho was breaking down the Kush buds when he suddenly stopped, looking up at Jynx.

"Fuck you still doing here? You want a piece of chicken to go?"

"I'm not hungry, but I do need to holla at chu, though."

"Make it fast."

Honcho didn't really care too much for Jynx. The only reason he kept him around was because he promised his father he'd take care of him when they were locked up together. Jynx wasn't good with money, hustling, or playing lookout. So, the next best thing for him to do was to simply run errands that kept him busy and out of his face.

"You're gonna wanna hear this."

"Speak on it."

"I take it you haven't heard about what happened to your man, Arkane?"

"Fuck happened to Arkane?" His brow furrowed, splitting open the cigar with the razorblade.

"He and his security got hit the other night." He reported, causing Honcho's brows to furrow further. "Cut down by assault rifles, the whole lot of 'em. Arkane was the only one left breathing."

"Thank Christ." Honcho looked relieved. He moved to cross his heart in the sign of the crucifix when the little man stopped him.

"But," he held up a finger, "he was run over twice. The second time his head was crushed like a rotten melon."

Honcho closed his eyes and lowered his head, massaging the bridge of his nose as he thought about what had been done to Arkane. He exhaled and looked back up at Jynx. "Who done this? And don't chu lie to me or I swear to Jesus Christ," he gritted his teeth and his eyes bulged angrily, "I'll carve out cha fucking liver and eat it right here in front of you!" He smacked his massive hand down on the desk top causing it to rattle.

"Him." Jynx said simply.

"Him?" Honcho's face contracted with confusion as he angled his head.

"The man that would not die."

"The man that would not die?" He massaged his chin as he thought of where he'd heard that before. His eyes lit up like twin chandeliers as the name struck inside of his head like a bolt of lightning. "Fearless."

"That's it." He sat up. "That's him, the one they call Fearless."

"Shiiieeet." Honcho smacked his hand back down on the desk top and looked away, thinking to himself. He looked back around to Jynx shaking his head. "I knew this shit was going to happen. Should've had this negrito eradicated a long time ago. Could've saved us all the headaches." He closed his eyes and hung his head, taking a deep breath. He ran a hand down his face and looked back up. "This cock sucker means business and I'll be damned if he walks away with me as another notch under his pinche belt.   Fuck   that."

"Ahem."

Honcho looked back around to find Jynx rubbing his index and thumb together. He picked right up on it. He wanted compensation for the information he'd laid on him. The Vato looked at him like he was stupid for even asking for payment. His large hand dipped inside of his desk drawer and when it came back up it was holding a Desert Eagle. He sat it on the table, clasped his hands under his chin and leaned forth.

He sniffed. "If I was you, I'd start making hurried steps toward that door." He nodded to the double doors of the exit. Jynx nodded, grabbed his apple jack and made for the door, slapping the hat upon his head.

"Piece of shit." The Mexican drug lord said under

his breath. His cell phone rang and he answered it. "What's up, Doll Face?"

"He's coming, he's coming for you Honcho." Melissa screamed frantically causing him to jump to his feet. Capaveli and La'Don came to stand by his desk with troubled looks on their faces.

"Wait, slow down." He frowned. "Who's coming for me?"

Ka-Boom!

An explosion went off that rocked the mansion.

*****

Two bright shining orbs moved hastily through the darkness heading for the entrance of the mansion. *Boom!* The vehicle plowed through the gates. The guards quickly formed a half circle before the flying vehicle. They pointed their M-16 rifles, closed one eye and caressed the trigger at the exact same time. The weapons bucked and vibrated in their hands spitting hot embers. Bullets chewed up the car, shattered the windshield, and burst the radiator. The car kept coming, with its music playing loud, it raged forward. It absorbed shot after shot until its tires were blown out and it slowed to a crawl, eventually stopping. The guards moved in slowly with their assault rifles pointed. If something jumped out of the vehicle alive, then they were going to make it dead.

The first guard approached the vehicle cautiously peering inside through the front passenger side window. He saw a bowie knife pinning the gas pedal to the floor. He listened to the busted radiator as well as Notorious B.I.G's *Come On*, which was playing inside…

Biggie Smalls, the millionaire, the mansion, the yacht/ The two weed spots, the two hot Glocks/ Haa! That's how I got the weed spot/ I shot dread in the head, took the bread and the land spread/ Lil' Gotti got the shotty to your body/ So don't resist, or you might miss Christmas/ I tote guns, I make number runs/ I give emcees the runs dripping
The rest of the guards surrounded the vehicle as the guard reached for the door-_handle. As soon as the door cracked open, the loud music infected the air, blaring loud and clear. He pulled the door open further and there was a *Ding,* his brow furrowed. He looked at the floor and saw a black device with red digital numbers on its screen. Two seconds were left on it.

I slay from far away/ Everybody hit the D-E-C-K
His eyes grew big and his mouth went to scream, but before the sound could escape the booby trapped car exploded. *Kaboom!* Severed arms, legs, backs and feet still inside of their shoes went high into the sky. The loose body parts came raining back down to the lawn along with crimson droplets, painting the rich green grass a different color.
Six more guards spilled out of the mansion with M-16s and itchy trigger fingers. Their faces were twisted as well as their lips. They were on some kill or be killed shit. Their eyes were so focused on the raging fire they didn't noticed Anton speed in. He balanced himself on the motorcycle, both arms erect, clutching the twin chrome handguns and letting them bitches go simultaneously.

Choot! Choot! Choot! Choot!!

"Gaaa!" "Ahhh!" "Gahhh!" "Arghhh!"

Embers ripped through the guards' chests, cheekbones and foreheads. Their faces displayed the agony they felt as their blood misted the air. The motorcycle played the same music that was playing inside of the car that   exploded
Come on mothafucka, come on (mothafucka)/ Come on mothafucka, come on (mothafucka)/ Come on mothafucka, come on (mothafucka) / Come on mothafucka, come on (mothafucka)

Choot! Choot!

With Biggie's last words said, the heads of the surviving guards disintegrated. The wind blew and carried microscopic pieces of brain and skull along with a crimson mist through the atmosphere. As soon as their bodies met with the lawn, Anton looked ahead at the front door. He spotted Honcho inside of the doorway, staring at him. He stood there for a time with a hard_-face just watching. It was as if he was paralyzed and he couldn't move. Anton shoved the bangers into the holsters on underneath his arms and revved up the motorcycle. The bike took off toward the mansion. Honcho slammed the door shut. Anton Popped a Willy on the sexy black machine, leaving the front wheel up. He zipped lined up the steps and rammed into the door, sending it slamming down on the floor.

The mansion was pitch black and motionless. There wasn't a sound save for the low hum of the motorcycle. Anton moved his head from left to right, looking through the dark tinted glass of the helmet's visor. Hearing a footstep at his left, he whipped his head back around and went for his holstered chrome thangs. Before he could draw them, a Mauri gator went slamming across his top. The helmet broke in halves and danced across the marble floor. The youngster went spilling to the surface. He was disoriented for a time, but he knew he had to act fast or be another R.I.P on a tombstone. With movements as fast as flashes, he drew both of his handguns. He was about to get it popping when Honcho descended upon him, kicking the shiny weapons from his hands and then him across the temple. The kick to the head left Anton dazed. He felt the Mexican kingpin's massive hand grasp him about the throat just as he was pulling the next trick out of his bag.

It seemed like Anton had pulled the mase out of thin air when he came around with it. The Southern gangster was so occupied with choking the life out of him that he wasn't aware of the impending pain he'd soon acknowledge. The youngster kneed him in the balls garnering a wail that seemed like it would fit more so coming from a wounded whale than a man. He grabbed his family jewels and the youngest of the Jackson kids took advantage. With both hands he swung the mase down into his right foot. *Thump!* The spiked metal ball of the mase stabbed through his leather gator. Honcho's eyes almost shot out of his head and his mouth stretched open so wide when he screamed his jaws ached.

"Ahhhhhhhhhh!" Red veins webbed his eyeballs and spittle flew from his mouth as his head trembled. Clenching his teeth, he fought back the jolts of excruciation that shot through his foot and moved to pull out the mase. While he was doing that, Anton was scrambling over toward one of his handguns. He'd almost had it in his hand when someone kicked it out of his reach. When he looked up, he met a kick square in the face that threw him on his back. Blood oozed out of his forehead and he looked up dizzily. Guns out by their sides, Capaveli and La' Don advanced on him. As Anton was getting upon his hands and knees they were tucking their burners. They pounced on him kicking and stomping him unmercifully.

"Haaa!" Honcho finally yanked the mase from out of his foot. He looked at the spiked metal ball and it was stained red with tiny pieces of his flesh clinging to it. He winced and looked to Anton as he was held up by his goons. He dropped the mase to the floor and limped over to him. Stopping before him, he watched his eyes roll into the back of his head and his mouth hang open as he moaned from   being   beaten.
"You lil' shit!" he snatched the burner off of Capaveli's waist and grabbed Anton by the lower half of his face. He squeezed his jaw so tightly his mouth opened like a fish. He then stuck the gun into his mouth until he heard him gag. "Goodnight."

Briiiiing! Briiiiing!

Honcho switched hands with the gun and used the other to pull the cell phone from off of his hip. He glanced at the screen and saw a very familiar number. He pressed answer and brought the cell phone to his ear.

"What's up? Yeah, that was me. I, uhhhh, had a situation here. I figured as much. I'll have my people clean things up ASAP. Well, hold 'em off, you're the goddamn chief of police! Now that's what I like to hear. Great! *Dick head,*" He said under his breath before disconnecting the call and placing the cell back on his hip. "Now where were we?"

"You were 'bout to pop this lil' nigga's top off." Capaveli reminded him, smacking Anton across the back of his head.

"Right." Honcho smiled sinisterly as he limped over to the barely conscious young man. He placed the gun under his chin and made to pull the trigger when he stalled at his bodyguard's request.

"Wait." La' Don blurted. "Shouldn't we probe this runt for the whereabouts of his homies?"

"Good thinking, Don. You always were a thinker." Honcho patted La'Don on his cheek and tucked the burner on his waist. He turned to Capaveli. "Call the boys and make sure they clean that mess up outside. And take his bike into the garage. Me and Don are gonna take this piece of shit down into the basement."

"Alright." Capaveli let La'Don scoop Anton into his arms.

An hour later…

"Fuuuckkkkk youuuuuuu!" A soaking wet Anton screamed loud enough to shattered glass with his eyes bulging and his head tilted back. He wrung himself of water as he danced around on the chain he hang bound from. Honcho stood off to the side with his arms folded across his chest watching unperturbed. Occasionally La' Don would spray the youngling with the water hose while Capaveli would zap him with the cattle prod.

"That's enough!" Honcho bellowed. His henchmen discontinued their routine and stepped aside. The Mexican kingpin limped in Anton's direction as he hung from the ceiling with his head bowed. His chest expanded and compressed with each breath he took. He was exhausted and hurting, but there wasn't any way in hell he would give up Eureka and Fear's whereabouts. Hell no, that would be the day someone would be able to say that he bitched up and ratted out. Never that, the gangsters that had a hand in raising him in the hood would look upon him with shame. Besides, that snitch shit just wasn't in his blood. The young nigga had never been loose with his lips.

"Look here, sport, you're either gonna give up your people or we're gonna Kentucky fry your lil' ass." Honcho promised, clenching the lower half of Anton's face as he stared into the whites of his eyes. "You copy that?"

"He who fears death—is in denial," he spoke weakly.

"Say what?" Honcho turned his ear toward Anton's lips.

"I said a coward dies one thousand deaths but a soldier dies only once."

"Made of steel," he spoke of the balls the youngster had for standing up to him. "You would have made an excellent gun, kid. It's just too bad you chose the wrong side." He let his chin drop to his chest and he stepped to Capaveli. He whispered something into his ear and he nodded. He then walked back over to where he'd been standing.

La'Don sprayed Anton down with the hose, making sure he was soaked. Capaveli pressed a button on the cattle-prod and it hummed eerily as electric volts surged through it. *Tak! Tak! Tak! Tak! Tak!* He was about to zap the little dude when he heard glass shattering and a loud thump as something hit the floor upstairs. Capaveli, La'Don and Honcho frowned as they exchanged glances.

"Check it out." Honcho told La'Don, throwing his head toward the staircase.

La'Don dropped the water hose and whipped his tool from his waist. Cautiously, he crept his way up the steps trying his best not to make a sound. Capaveli and Honcho listened closely hearing the doorknob being turned and the door being opened. There wasn't a sound to be heard and all seemed to be calm until.

Thoomp!
"Gaahhh!"
Thoomp!
Thoomp!

"La' Don! La'Don!" Capaveli called out but he

didn't receive an answer. He went to head for the staircase and there was a loud racket. La'Don came tumbling down the steps hard and fast. He slid across the floor and bumped into the washer. He was wearing three arrows. One in his chest, sternum, and heart. His eyes were staring off to the side and his lips were partially apart. Capaveli and Honcho wore expressions of surprise on their faces. They exchanged glances. Honcho threw his head toward the staircase which was his way of telling him to head up the stairs to see what was going on.

Capaveli swallowed hard and set the cattle prod down on the dryer. He brandished his banger as he crept toward the staircase. He stepped over a lifeless La'Don and snuck up the staircase, causing the steps to squeak with each step he took. Honcho watched him attentively and hoped he could dispatch whoever was up there waiting.

Blocka! Blocka! Blocka!

The suddenly burst of gunfire startled Honcho and he ducked behind Anton, pressing his gun against the back of his dome. He peered over his shoulder and watched for what would happen next.

Thoomp!

"Arghhhh!"

Thoomp!

Capaveli came tumbling down the steps just as La'Don had. He reached the end of the steps lying in an awkward position. He sported an arrowed through the eye and one through the chest.

After the goon went falling down the stairs everything else fell quiet. The silence was driving Honcho mad. He needed some noise, any noise that would make him feel at ease.

"Who's there? Who the fuck are you?" The Mexican gangster hollered out, hiding behind Anton ready to send a bullet through the back of his head and out of his face.

For a while there was silence and then a voice spoke aloud.
"Death!"
"Oh, yeah? Well, come get me mothafucka, I've been waiting!" Honcho spat, sweat rolling down his forehead and the sides of his face.
The lights went out.
"Huh?" He looked around worried. The basement was dark. The only light was the one illuminating from the small window that nearly reached the ceiling.
"Let the kid go!"
"I'll let 'em go alright, straight to hell once I put a hot one through his skull." He fumed and breathed heavily. The hot air from his nose and mouth moistened the back of Anton's neck.
"I'm only gonna say that once!"
"Fuck you!" he shot back. "I'm only gonna say that once!"
"Reka!" Fear called out.
Honcho's eyes narrowed and he whipped around to the small window. Someone was there behind the glass, but he couldn't make them out. However, he did take note of the silenced gun they had aimed at him. Two bullets whizzed through the glass and struck the muscle headed Vato in the chest. Confusion captivated his face and he looked down at the two expanding red dots that were there. He went to take a shot at Eureka when suddenly Anton whipped around, wrapping his legs around his neck. He

gritted his teeth and squeezed with all of his might. Honcho's eyes grew big and red veins quickly formed in them as his mouth fell open. His tongue inched out as he gagged and struggled to breathe. He dropped his gun and it clasped when it hit the floor. Using both hands, he tried to pry the youngster's legs from around his neck. The more he put up a fight was the tighter Anton squeezed. Honcho gagged as he clawed at his legs but then abruptly it happened, his head whipped to the right violently.

Snappp!
The Cholo's eyes rolled to their corners and he went limp while wrapped in the boy's limbs. Anton held tightly to him a while longer before releasing him. He dropped to his knees and hit the floor harder than a mothafucka, dead.

The Jackson's second born slumped on the chain and hollered out, "Y'all come down. They're all dead!"

Fear came hurrying down the steps with a bow gun and Eureka on his heels. He took a gander at Capaveli and La'Don's dead bodies as he stepped over them en route to Anton. Sitting the bow gun down, he grabbed the little nigga by his legs and hoisted him up, slipping the chain that bounded his wrists from over the hook in the ceiling. He held him in his arms like a husband would his wife over a threshold.

"How—how did you find me?" Anton asked weakly, behind hooded eyes.

"There's a GPS system on the motorcycle." Fear informed him.

"See?" Eureka showed him the screen of the black device in her hand. There was a map on the display with a green dot that flashed rapidly, making a beeping sound.

"Oh." Anton head dropped, he was out cold.

"Come on. Let's get 'em home."

CHAPTER TEN
Hours later…

"That was a real bonehead move you made." Eureka spoke to her baby brother from the edge of the bed. He was lying on his back with his arms folded across his chest.

"I did what I had to do for the good of the team," Anton reasoned. "Besides, I laid a lot of them boys out. I almost took out cha boy Honcho too, but he caught wind of me coming."

"You and your stubborn, arrogant ass!" Eureka fumed. "You could have gotten yourself killed and then what, huh?" She wiped the tears that brewed and ran from the corners of her eyes.

"Would have, could have, but I didn't."

"If it wasn't for me and Fear arriving when we did, there's no telling what would have happened." Tears ran down her cheeks and she wiped them away. He sat up in bed, hating to see her in that state. There was something about her tears that did something to him. For as hard as he was, the sight of seeing the only thing he loved in pain hurt more than being stabbed in the back by his best friend.

"Reka, I'm sor.—" He reached for her, but she smacked his hand away, violently.

"No, what if you would have gotten killed tonight?" She shot to her feet, nostril flaring and eyes filling with moisture. "Where would that have left me, Ant? Alone! All by myself."

*****

It was the night of Giselle's 30th birthday. A half-eaten chocolate cake, paper plates with crumbs, half empty

144

soda cans and beer bottles littered the coffee table. She smiled and giggled, occasionally covering her mouth with her hands. She was feeling the love in that moment and her family was making sure of it. Snoop Doggy Dog's 'Beautiful' blared from the stereos speakers. Bootsy was holding the mop handle singing into it while a younger Eureka and Anton were sharing the broom handle. Together they were crooning the lyric of the song to the birthday girl, moving to the sound of the music.

Beautiful, I just want you to know (Oh, hoo)/ You're my favorite girl (Ehh, oh yeah, there's something about you)/ See I just want you to know/ That you are really special/ Ohh why, oh why, oh why, oh why?
Bootsy continued to sing, ignorant to the fact that his children were playing Tug-O-War over the broom's handle.
"Stop hogging it, Ant!" Eureka pulled, her face was twisted into a scowl.

"I had it first, stupid!" Anton frowned, pulling it back.
"You're stupid!"

"You're stupid!"

They went back and forth for a time. Eureka held the handle of the broom tightly. When Anton went to pull the broom back she let it go and he went sailing back, falling up against the wall. This stole their parents' attention. The music was still going when Anton jumped up and slugged his sister in the chest. She reacted by punching him in the head. He stumbled backwards but quickly righted himself.

"*Aye, y'all stop that shit!*" *Giselle said from the couch.*

Anton's face morphed into something ugly as he rushed his sister, cocking back his fist about to swing. Before the young boy could connect he was snatched up by his father. He tossed him on the couch along with his sister.

Ringgggg!

The telephone had rung and Giselle rose, excusing herself. "*Let me answer this phone. Thank you, baby.*" *She kissed her husband on the lips as she passed him, thanking him for the party and concert he and the kids had put on for her.*

"*What the hell is the matter with y'all fighting each other?*" *Bootsy asked, kneeled before his children. His eyebrows were arched and his forehead wrinkled.*

"*She started it, Dad!*" *Anton told him, giving his sister the evil eye.*

"*I started it?*" *she said with a raised eyebrow and a finger to her chest.* "*We were supposed to be sharing but you were trying to hog it.*"

"*I had...*" *Anton was cut short by their father's interjecting.*

"*Stop! Stop! Stop!*" *Bootsy words grew higher in octaves.*

He looked between his children with a stern look, motioning a finger.

"*If I ever see or hear about you two fighting again, I'ma whip you 'til my arms falls off, you hear?*" *He looked at them with dead serious eyes. They hung their heads unable to look him in the face. He was masculine with a*

slight build, and a deep voice, easily intimidating to a pair of   *kids.*
"Yes, Dad." Anton looked into his eyes like he'd been taught to address men.
"Yes, Daddy." Eureka responded, meeting her father's gaze.
Bootsy placed his children's hands into each other's palms, squeezing them closed.
"Y'all listen up," Bootsy cleared his throat before he began. "One day there's going to come a time when me and your mother won't be here. When that day comes all you guys will have in this world is one another. That's all. You," he pointed to Eureka, "You look out for your baby brother. You don't let anything happen to him that don't happen to you first. You understand me, baby girl?" She nodded yes. He pointed to his boy. "You, do the same for your sister. Don't let any harm come to her that doesn't come to you first. You are one another's keepers. Do you understand me, champ?" He nodded yes. "There is no tie on this earth stronger than blood. Family is very important. You protect your own at all costs." The Jackson kids nodded in agreement. "Alright, ya'll apologize to one another."
"Sorry, Reka," Anton said honesty.
"Sorry, Ant," Eureka replied truthfully.
They hugged.
Bootsy smiled. "Can your Daddy get some of that love, too?"
The siblings smiled brightly and hugged their father. He closed his eyes as he rubbed their backs enjoying   the   moment.
"I love you, Dad."
"I love you, Daddy." Eureka said afterwards.

"I love y'all, too." *He kissed them both on the sides of their faces.*

*****

Anton hung his head shamefully, thinking about getting killed and leaving his sister alone.

"You didn't think about that, did you? You were only thinking about yourself! You were being selfish!" Eureka breathed heavily, bottom lip quivering. She was upset. They already lost both parents so to lose one another would be devastating. The thought of losing her brother scared the shit out of her. She couldn't imagine living in a world without him. She'd much rather die beside him on a mission, both guns up blazing. At least that way they'd be together because a life without baby boy wasn't a life at all.

He looked up at her with regretful eyes, rising from off of the bed and approaching.

"Please, don't cry, Reka, I'm sorry. I really am." He spoke the truth.

"That was stupid, Anton, so fucking stupid." Her voice trembled as she wiped her eyes.

"I know, will you forgive me?" He opened his arms for a hug.

She didn't say a word. She fell into him and wrapped her arms around him, squeezing him tightly.

"I forgive you but if you ever do something like thiatagain, I'll kill you myself, you hear me?" She held him at arm's length, looking into his eyes. He nodded *yes*. "I love you too much to lose you, we're all we've got, baby brother."

She hugged him again, tighter this time. She was so happy they were able to rescue him in time because God knew if something would have happened to him, she would have burned the city down to ashes until she felt his death had been avenged.

"Ahem."

Still wrapped in one another's arms, the siblings looked to the door. Fear was there wrapping his black leather whip around his arm. Anton already knew what was cracking then, he didn't need to ask. He was disobedient in his going against the killer's orders, just as Constance had. He had to answer for the violation.

Anton looked back to his sister and broke their embrace.

"I've gotta go."

"Fear, wait, no one got killed. Maybe we can let 'em slide this…"

"No," Anton shook his head. "No one is above L.O.E, not even its leader."

"Fear…" She looked at him with pleading eyes, hoping that he'd change his mind. Anton left the bedroom leaving Fear and Eureka alone. The assassin watched the youngster journey down the hall for a second before focusing his attention back on the boy's sister.

He held her gaze for a moment. "No one." In reference to no one being above Loyalty Over Everything. After speaking his peace, he left the bedroom and headed down the hall.

Eureka sat down on the bed and hung her head as she fidgeted with her fingers. Her head shot up when she heard her brother's muffled screams as the leather whip licked at his back. She could literally hear the whip whistling through the air and landing across his bare skin. Slowly she began to cry, trickles splashing on her lap and knees. She wiped her face with the back of her hand and continued to listen. Once the tenth lash had landed, she broke downstairs to comfort her brother and made sure he was okay.

*****

Crunch pulled up in front of one of many of Malvo's spots and murdered the engine. He settled back in his seat and leaned his head back against the headrest, closing his eyes. What Ronny had said to him had been weighing heavily on his mind. He only hoped his closest friend was wrong about the man that had raised them from pups to dogs. God knew if his allegations turned out to be true, he wouldn't be able to look himself in the mirror anymore. How could he stomach his own reflection after what he'd let go down between Malvo and Antoinette? The act was despicable and it should have never happened. Even if Ronny did do some shady shit, there were other measures that could have been taken to get back at him. Making a man pay for his trifling ways was one thing but seeking retribution from his family was another.

Crunch exhaled and ran both of his hands down his face. He stuck his keys into his pocket and popped the trunk. He opened the trunk and took a cautious scan of his whereabouts before retrieving two hefty duffle bags. He closed the trunk with his elbow and headed up the stairs of the house. He dropped one of the bags at his foot and knocked on the door in a very specific pattern. He saw someone peek through the curtains and heard muffled voices coming from the other side of the door. There was the mention of his name and then the locks being undone. The front door was opened by a skinny light skinned nigga rocking a doo-rag and a Rams football jersey. His hand was curled around the handle of a .380.

"What's up, my nigga?" Doo-rag asked.

"Ain't shit, Boss Dawg get here yet?" He asked as he crossed the threshold.

"Yeah, big homie is in the back room." He answered closing and locking door.

Crunch was quickly overwhelmed by the thick weed fog as soon as he entered the house. The smoke was so thick you would have thought that it was the aftermath of an explosion. Looking to his left, he found another one of the workers in front of a fifty-five inch flat-screen TV. One hand held tight to a PS4 controller while the other had a thin blunt wedged between his fingers. He took the occasional pull from the L as he waited for his homeboy to return. The game was on pause and he was ready to finish whopping on his ass in Madden.

"What's up, C?" The worker called out.

"What's cracking?" Crunch threw his head back.

"Nothing. Just finna finish spanking on this fool in Madden."

"That's what's up," Crunch replied.

"Nigga you ain't spanking jack shit." Doo-rag interjected, taking the blunt from him. "You up by seven points, you act like you're blowing me out or something."

He grabbed the controller and plopped down on the couch. He un-paused the game and they got back to it.

"Yooooooo," Crunch called out once he'd reached the door of Malvo's homemade office.

"Who that?" Malvo hollered back.

"Crunch."

"Come in. It's open." Malvo told him.

Crunch entered the office to find Malvo sitting behind his deck holding an automatic shotgun up at his shoulder and staring at a portrait. His cheeks were damp and his eyes were glassy, so he knew that he'd been crying. He couldn't blame him, though. He was sure he would have been just as torn up as he was had it been his family that had been murdered in cold blood. Even after they had terrorized Siska's establishments and laid down a couple of his people it still did little to ease his pain. After his tragedy he wasn't sure if his boss would ever be the same, he could only pray with each day that passed that his pain lessened.

When Malvo kissed the portrait Crunch knew it had to have been a photograph of his family. He watched him place the portrait inside of the desk drawer and pull out two pens, two notepads, two calculators and a money counter machine. He sat these items on the desk top and propped his shotgun against the desk on the floor.

"You hear about this nigga, Ronny, out here killing my people and setting fire to my traps?" Malvo questioned Crunch.

Damn, that nigga Ronny ain't playing no games, Crunch thought. *He's really bringing it.*

"Nah," his face contracted with a look of surprise.

"Yeah, he killed that nigga Woo, Skooter, and Rick," Malvo reported. "The only nigga he left alive was Doc and that's so he could tell me that he did it. You know what this means, right?" He didn't wait for him to respond before continuing. "War, I'ma bring it to any and every mothafucka out here that's gotta problem with Malvo. That's on my wife and my baby, straight up." He spoke with a dead serious look in his eyes.

Crunch stared at the floor just nodding his head.

"Anyway, I'm just letting you know what's up." Malvo smacked and rubbed his hands together. "Let's get to counting up these bands."

He then watched as Crunch dumped the contents of each duffle bag out on the desk top. The two of them went right to work counting up all of the money. Once they were done, they secured the bills with beige rubber bands and sat the stacks of them neatly on the desk top. They then lay back in their respective black leather executive office chairs passing a blunt between them.

"Soooo, you want me to make that other run tonight, right?" Crunch blew smoke out of the corner of his mouth as he passed the L back. He was speaking up on the new plug had been laced with. It was him that had been making the exchange as of late. He had twice the responsibility since Ronny wasn't any longer in the picture. He wasn't studying it, though, because he was getting broken off something lovely.

"Yep," Malvo responded. He took the blunt and glanced at his titanium Rolex. "He's expecting you in about an hour."

Crunch glanced at the time on his cell phone's screen and stuck it into his pocket.

"Well, shit, I may as well bust that move right now then." He rose up from off of the chair and grabbed one of the empty duffle bags. He made to toss some of the stacks of money into the bag when Malvo stopped him.

"Hold up."

"What's up?" Crunch frowned.

"I ain't tryna give that wetback this new paper I made." He claimed, picking up a duffle bag from behind his desk and slinging it over to him, "Out with the old in with the new."

Crunch unzipped the duffle bag and peered inside. A surprised expression crossed his face and his heart sunk into the pit of his stomach. Inside there were stacks of money secured by blue rubber bands. The same blue rubber banded stacks of money Ronny had warned him about.

The money will more than likely have blue rubber-bands around it." He remembered him saying. *"I think that's how he separates the real from the fake. "*

He heard his road dawg's voice inside of his head, each time it got deeper and deeper. As if it was being said by some demonic entity.

"Something wrong, my nigga?" Malvo's forehead crinkled, as he took in the look on his capo's face.

Crunch mustered up a counterfeit smile, "Nothing. We're good." He then zipped the bag up, dapped up his man and headed for the door. He opened up the door and was about to step through it when he was called back. "Yeah?"

"I love you, C. You're like a son to me. Ronny, too." He tapped his fist to his chest.

Crunch tapped his fist to his chest and made his exit.

*****

Three men lay on their stomach gagged with their wrists bound behind their back. They stared up at the man that had them in a fucked up situation. They had tears pooling in their eyes and their bodies were trembling, for good reason too. Their lives rested in the hands of one man. Ronny Montgomery.

Ronny walked around the living room dousing everything with gasoline along with Nicolay and Mikhail.

Once the Russians had finished they tossed their gas cans aside and shook up cans of spray paint as they headed for the door. Ronny stood over the trap boys whistling as he poured gasoline over their bodies and head. The men squeezed their eyes shut and shook their heads, blowing their noses as the overwhelming odor of gasoline burned their nostrils. They gagged and huffed feeling the fumes of the flammable liquid invading their lungs, threatening to poison them. Ronny stopped whistling and dropped the gas can on one of their heads. It bounced off of it and tumbled over onto the floor. He walked over to the coffee table where wrinkled stacks of money, a block of heroin, and four black handguns resided. He grabbed a stack of the money and the block of heroin, holding them up so the men could see them.

"Y'all see," The men peered up at him through narrowed eyes, trying to keep the gasoline out of them. "Y'all know what this is right? Dope!" He looked at the stack of money and the block of heroin. "Now y'all probably think that this is what this is all about, but you're wrong, 'cause I don't give a fuck about none of this shit! All I want is that nigga, Malvo, so y'all either gon' tell me where he is or there's gonna be a lil' barbeque in the hood." He looked around at all of the faces of the men. They reeked of fear. But their tears didn't mean anything to him. As far as he was concerned, they were all guilty by association.

The men squirmed and screamed as they twisted their heads, back and forth. They were all trying to say something at the same time but the duct tape over their mouths restrained the sound.

"Y'all got something y'all want to tell me?" he asked as he held the flame of a lighter to the stack of money, setting it on fire. The men winced and screamed at the top of their lungs with the duct tape muffling the sound. Ronny snatched the tape off of each of their mouths. They all gave him promises of not knowing where Malvo was and how they didn't have anything to do with what had gone down between them.

Ronny made a face and shook his head. The men were still complaining when he tossed the burning stack of dead white men on them. The living room went up in flames quickly, spreading throughout the house like gossip in the tabloids. The men danced on the floor screaming, shouting and hollering. Ronny plucked a half smoked blunt from the ashtray off of the coffee table. He headed out of the house sticking the L between his lips like he didn't hear the brutal screams of the men he'd set on fire. He was halfway out of the yard when he fired up and took a couple puffs. He started back walking and by the time he reached the gate, the house exploded with a golden orange light. Fire erupted out of the windows, sending flames and broken glass rushing out into the night's air.

The house was well lit by the raging fire, so much so you could see what the Russians had sprayed on the front of it: *Malvo, come out, come out, wherever you are!*

Ronny meant it when he said he wasn't going to stop until he got his hands on Malvo. It may not be tomorrow or the next day, but one day his ass would be his.

CHAPTER ELEVEN

"I know goddamn well you aren't sitting here crying your eyes out over that piece of shit?" Bemmy spoke to his daughter from the opposite side of the table of the restaurant he owned. The only persons present were them, his two bodyguards and the chef. It had been a while since he'd gotten the chance to just sit down and chop it up with his   baby   girl.

Bemmy knew he didn't have any business being out that night in the public eye. He had one of the most dangerous men to have ever wielded a gun with his sight set on his soul and he was determined to get it. Despite all of this, he still decided to step out for a night on the town with his daughter. See, in the streets Niles Bemmy was looked at as a man of power and sophistication.

So, if he went into hiding on the account of some killer being after him, then niggaz would be looking at him suspiciously. He couldn't have that because it was shit like that *that* could tarnish a man of his caliber's reputation. He had to save face, so here he was inside of his own restaurant enjoying his favorite dish.

Annabelle sat with her head hung wiping her dripping tears with a cloth napkin. She was a pretty chocolate girl with thick hair she wore in Shirley Temple curls. She wore pearls, a sleeveless white dress with a thick gold belt around her waist. Annabelle was a college student with a bright future. Her only weakness were assholes.

"No," she replied sheepishly.

"I can't fucking believe this." He spoke under his breath with a jaw full of steak as he cut it into cubes on his plate. "You feel sorry for a nigga that beats on you and treats you like a door mat? That's weak, and I didn't raise you to be such." He shook his head as he picked up his glass of red wine, taking a sip. He smacked his lips as he savored the fine taste, looking upon the glass as if it held the tastiest beverage known to man. He sat the glass back down and continued with the devouring of his meal.

"Daddy." Annabelle sniffled, patting her eyes dry. He threw his head back a little like *yeah?* as he chewed his food. "Just tell me, is he—I he dead?"

Bemmy looked up from his plate and gave her a look that clarified it. She broke down sobbing, falling out of her chair and performing like a mother at her son's funeral. The OG exhaled and sipped a little more wine.

"Leman." He called on his bodyguard.

"Yes, sir?"

"Take her out to the car and have the chauffer take her home. I'll have Lex call us up another car."

"Yes sir." Leman got Annabelle to her feet and helped her out to the limousine. Once he'd seen her off, he made his way back inside of the restaurant. He was just in time to see his boss dropping a couple of bills on the chef before he left for the night.

The OG patted the chef on his back and told him goodnight. He consumed the last of his meal and wiped his mouth, dropping the cloth napkin on the table. When he stood to his feet Leman helped him slip on his suit's jacket. He smoothed out his wrinkled jacket and buttoned it at the waist.

Lex's cell phone rang and he answered it. Not long after he was disconnecting the call.

"That was the chauffer. The car's parked out front."

"Good," Bemmy replied. "You make sure everything was locked up?"

"Yes, sir, Mr. Bemmy."

Right then they heard a voice boom around them.

"Niles!" The name echoed over the loud speaker, clenching everyone's heart like strong hands. Bemmy's head snapped in each and every direction. His bodyguards stepped closer to him, pulling their guns and getting ready for the impending drama. They were on high alert too, necks moving about.

"Niles mothafucking Bemmy, are you ready to die, nigga?" The voice echoed again.

"Lex, you check the front!" Bemmy ordered one guard. "Leman, you check the back, and watch cho ass, nigga! First man to bring me that son of a bitch's head gets a blank check, you write your price."

"Got cha, boss, we're on it." Leman left to carry out his instructions.

"We'll get 'em, Mr. Bemmy. You can count on that." Lex added his two cents.

As soon as the suits departed the lights flickered and went out. Then the backup generators kicked in storing dim lighting to the establishment. Bemmy's heart was beating madly inside of his chest. He could literally feel each time it thumped up against his breastbone. He whipped out an asthma pump and shook it up as he looked around terrified. He sprayed two gusts into his mouth and tried to calm down. He had begun to relax a little when he heard...

"Arghhhhhh!"

"Leman! Lemannn! What the fuck happened, man?" He called out to the back of the restaurant. He waited to hear a response but all he got in return was Lex's scream,

"Ahhhhhh!"

He whipped around, calling out his name but he never replied. Propping his foot on a nearby chair, he lifted the leg of his slacks and pulled a small caliber pistol free from his ankle holster. He held the gun up at his shoulder and when he turned around something hard slammed into his chest. He heard a thud and then felt tumbling on the floor. He looked up and saw a severed head rolling up from him, it belonged to Leman. The eyes were as wide as they could be and the mouth was stuck open, like he was screaming before he was murdered. His pupils stared up at his boss accusingly. Hearing a glass shatter nearby, the OG spun around with his finger resting on the trigger. He squeezed off with rapid succession. *Bop! Bop! Bop!* No one was there. He looked to the floor and saw a broken wine glass. Sweat beaded and slipped down his forehead. He swallowed spit as his head snapped in every direction. His breathing was heavy and anxiety had tighten his chest so much that it felt like someone was squeezing his heart in the palm of their hand.

"Old ass nigga!" The voice echoed.

The old school gangster moved about the restaurant with his neck on a swivel, sweeping his small black pistol around. He was paranoid and ready to put something hot into any opposing threat. He wiped his wet forehead with the back of his hand and continued to take a cautious scan of the establishment. He looked over his shoulder and saw someone in a black hoodie and Timbs. He whipped around and gripped his pistol with both hands, pulling the trigger.

Bop! Bop! Bop!

The floor to ceiling windows shattered and sparks deflected off of the metal shutters as they came down to seal the establishment. The cat wearing the hoodie and

Timbs howled in pain, catching one in the leg and falling to the ground. Bemmy continued to squeeze the trigger until he heard his weapon click. He looked to the gun and tossed it   aside.

"You ready to die, old man?" The voice echoed again over the loud speaker.

"Huh?" Bemmy turned around in circles, forehead beaded with sweat as he scanned his surroundings. His eyes were as big as golf balls and his mouth was stuck open. His mouth was as dry as cotton so he swallowed his spit, trying to wet his esophagus with his saliva. All he could hear was his heart pounding in his ears and his own heavy breathing. Death was coming for him. He could feel it. It was like a woman's intuition.

There was a thud and the rattling of dishes as if something heavy had landed on a table at his rear. He spun around to find a dark hooded figure standing up on one of the tables. He stared up at the figure as he slowly took steps backwards toward the corridor that lead to the backdoor exit of the restaurant. His face was shiny and dripping with sweat at this time. Once he reached the beginning of the hall, he whipped around and hauled ass. He ran as fast as he could, glancing over his shoulder as he made a mad dash. Seeing the figure darken the beginning of the corridor, he panicked and ran even faster. He was so focused on him as he was moving that he didn't pay any attention to what was ahead.

"Yuckkkk!" Bemmy's eyeballs almost leaped out of his head as his mouth shot open. His pupils rolled up toward his forehead where they found a knife halfway buried in his skull. "Gaggggaaa!" He staggered back bumping against the wall. A short man approached, taking an easy stroll like he was out for a late night walk. He pulled off his hood and revealed a pair of grisly eyes and a heinous smile.

"What I tell you, old man?" Fear looked his victim in the eyes. He pulled up the see through mask he was wearing. He chuckled and bit down on his bottom lip, observing his handiwork. "That's your ass!" He held Bemmy's hand against the wall and drove a knife through it, pinning it against the wall. He did the same to his other hand and pulled a third knife from his sleeve. *Snikt!* He flipped the knife over in his palm and grabbed him by the neck.

"Gaaaa." Drool pooled inside of the OG's mouth and spilled down the killer's gloved hand.

Fear's face tightened with malice and his jaws clenched. With a grunt, he drove the last knife into Bemmy's open mouth. The knife pierced the back of his neck and pinned his head against the wall. His eyes rolled completely to their whites and his lips moved animatedly for a time before remaining stuck. He expelled his last breath then slumped, hanging against the wall. Fear observed the work he had put in proudly, like a man that had built something with his own two hands.

Eureka approached with Anton bringing up the rear, limping along. They pulled the hoods from their heads and revealed the see through masks they were wearing. The siblings took up space beside their mentor, taking a good look at his latest kill as if it were a Picasso painting hanging on the wall.

"Game over." Fear sneered and harped up a glob of spit, hawking it in Bemmy's still face. It splattered against his forehead, slid down and dripped off his eyebrow. "Let's get the fuck outta here."

*****

Malvo pulled into the driveway and bodied his truck. He took a minute to think to himself before opening the glove box and removing his gun. He tested the weight of the heavy metal weapon, lightly bouncing it up and down in his palm. He then pressed it underneath his chin, squeezing his eyes shut and swallowing his spit. He sat his finger on the trigger, huffing and puffing as he tried to build up the courage to end his life. His huffing and puffing grew louder and louder as tears ran down his cheeks. His finger slowly compressed on the trigger and he licked his ashy lips. One hug of the trigger and all of his pain and suffering would come to an end. And then finally, he would be reunited with his wife and daughter. Oh, how he yearned to see that beautiful smile stretched across his baby girl's face. To hear her call him daddy and wrap her little arms around his neck and kiss him on the cheek. He couldn't wait to feel the warm flesh of his wife's body as she lay pressed against him. The scent of her perfume, the taste of her lips, the loving look in her eyes when he used to stare into her face. One shot, one kill, and he could be right there with them. It was so easy, and that was the exact reason why he wasn't going to do it. Suicide would be the weak way out and there wasn't shit soft about him.

He took the tool from his underneath his chin and wiped his face with the sleeve of his leather jacket. He then popped the trunk and recovered the duffle bags.

Malvo came through the door and dropped his duffle bags off by the coat stand. He hung up his jacket and made his way for the kitchen to make himself a drink. He flipped on the light switch and was stunned when he saw who it was waiting for him.

"What the hell are you doing here?" The creases of his forehead deepened when he saw Crunch sitting at the kitchen table. One hand was lying flat on the table top while the other was dangling at his side. His eyes were glassy and bloodshot as he peered up at the man he considered his father. You could tell that he was crying from the white streaks sprawled down his cheeks. Seeing this look in his eyes made the big man uneasy. He wanted to try for his banger which was tucked at the small of his back but he didn't want to catch one in his back like J Rock in the South Central movie.

"You've lied, you've manipulated and you've taken advantage of everyone who has ever showed love for you." The jet black hoodlum put it out there. Once he got the money to buy the dope with, he shot straight over to Office Depot and bought that special pen that could tell whether the money was real or not. It wasn't.

"Wha—what are you talking about?" Malvo played stupid. "I—"

"Shhhhhh," Crunch closed his eyes as he held a finger to his lips, hushing him. His eyelids slowly peeled open and his eyes settled back on him. He reached inside of the pocket of his jacket and pulled out something, smacking it flat down on the table top. His ashy calloused hand moved back and unveiled what it was covering, a counterfeit hundred dollar bill with a black mark on it. Malvo's eyes darted down to the bill. He was stunned, *how in the fuck did he figure it out?*

Ah shit, he thought, closing his eyes and massaging the bridge of his nose. He didn't know how he was going to get his chunky ass out of this one but he had to think fast. He shrugged, "Big deal, it's just a hundred dollar—"

"Don't lie to me, nigga!" Crunch shouted, his nostrils pulsating, chest inflating and deflating. He was in a blind rage. The nigga he loved like he'd shot him out of his own nut sack had turned him against a cat that was as good as his blood brother. He had used a tool against him he had been lacking since the day he was pushed out of his mother's womb and took his first breath of air. "I'm sick of all of your lies! Your deceit! Your fuckery!" He drew his ratchet. He pointed it at Malvo and his meaty hands shot up. He was wide eyed as he wondered if that gun was going to give him some plastic surgery.

"Crunch, you need to…"

Boc!

Malvo clutched the spewing hole in his leg. Blood seeped between his fingers. "Arghhh." He grimaced and clenched his teeth.

"Don't chu ever tell me what I need to do! You aren't the boss of me!"

Boc!

One through the thigh.

Boc!

A second through the arm.

"Gaaaa, fuck!" He turned around to run. A hot rock whizzed above his head and another one sent debris flying from the doorway. Crunch came from around the table, arm extended and gun at the ready as he stalked his former employer. Malvo hobbled a couple of feet before crumpling like a brown paper bag. He turned over on his back. Looking beyond his Timberland boots he saw his street son approaching, gun smoking. He let his head fall back against the floor and stared up at his assailant as he came to stand over him. His ratchet pointed in his face, eyes moist and pink as if he'd been crying after the loss of his father. He wasn't gone yet but one well-placed bullet and he would be.

"I loved you, man!" He wiped the trailing tears from his face with the back of his hand, but was sure to keep his banger pointed down at Malvo's face. He locked eyes with the only man that he'd ever considered a father. It seemed like a decade had passed in that moment, a decade of thinking that led him to his final conclusion. He couldn't bring himself to do it. He let his arm fall to his side and stepped over him, heading for the door. Malvo's eyes peeled open and he looked all around, settling on the door that Crunch had just disappeared through. His head dropped back down to the floor and he closed his eyes thanking God for sparing his life once again.

He felt a vibration and heard a faint tune against his side. Reaching inside of his leather jacket, he pulled free his cell phone and flipped it open. "Hello?" he grimaced. "Great, uh, nothing, I'm fine. Give. Me. The address. No, I'll remember it." After mentally recording the address he was being given, he flipped the cell closed and struggled to get upon his feet. He tore a bed sheet into strips and tied up his wounds to slow his bleeding. He then made a homemade splint for his leg.

Malvo knew that the walls were closing in on him. He not only had Ronny, the Russians, Eureka and Anton looking to claim his life but now he had Crunch on his back as well. Although he'd spared his life who's to say that he wouldn't have a change of heart and come back for him?

You fucked up not finishing me off, homeboy, he thought, as he headed for the door. *I ain't even got to get at you. A nigga money is long, I'ma send a couple of them wolves at cha. You can count on that, just as soon as I'm done with this Eureka business.*

With that done, he made his way out of his house. He had a date with Eureka Jackson.

*****

"I appreciate you stopping by on such a short notice, family." Fear slapped hands with the doctor that had come out to patch up Anton.

"Don't worry about it," the doctor adjusted his glasses. "Let's just call it a favor between friends."

"You got it." He opened the door and patted the good doctor on his back as he headed out of the door.

"How is baby boy?" Eureka asked concerned.

"He's gonna be fine," Fear answered. "He removed the bullet and patched 'em up. He left some pain killers and some antibiotics too."

"What is he in there doing?"

"Sleeping."

Eureka focused her attention back on the flat screen TV. She was watching a rerun of The Shield.

"Baby brother had a rough day."

"Yeah. Well, I'm gonna go crash." He leaned over the sofa and pecked her lips before advancing through the hall.

"I'll be in there in a minute."

"Alright," he said, before disappearing into the corridor.

A knock at the door drew Eureka's attention. She picked her Glock up from off of the glass coffee table and approached the front door. She took a gander through the curtains just in time to see the smoke from the exhaust pipes of a speeding car. Eureka unchained and unlocked the door. She stood off to the side and turned the knob, snatching it open. She stood where she was gripping her banger at her waist firmly. She swung into the doorway with her gun extended ready to let it ring. Her forehead creased and she narrowed her eyes when she didn't see anyone. She looked down and saw a burgundy wood stained coffin big enough to fit a new born baby. There were chunks of ground and dirt remnants over it and the porch.

Eureka stepped out onto the porch, looking up and down the street. She lightly kicked the coffin. When nothing happened, she tucked her weapon and got down on her knees. She placed her ear against the door of the coffin and listened, trying to see if there was ticking which would indicate that there was a time bomb inside. Figuring that it was safe, she picked the coffin up and gave another scan of the block before ducking back inside. She kicked the front door closed and carried the coffin over to the coffee table. She carefully opened it and was surprised to see what she found: a DVD inside of a jewel case taped down to the floor of it. The skin on her forehead bunched together wondering what the hell the DVD could be. She snatched the jewel case free of the tape and opened it, inserting it into the DVD player. The flat screen turned on instantly.

She saw someone handcuffed to a pipe inside of a dimly lit boiler room that looked like her mother, so Eureka leaned forward and narrowed her eyes trying to see if her eyes were deceiving her.

"Mommy?" she uttered once she realized it was the woman that had pushed her out into the cold, cruel world. Lines deepened on her forehead and she angled her head once she saw Constance enter the frame. She gave her mother an ass whipping that made her cringe and turn her head. The assault left her mother on her hand and knees.

Constance stood back in a fighting stance, chest heaving and still ready for some more action. She wore a wicked expression. She was enjoying every bit of the brutality she was dispensing. It seemed to make her nipples hard.

Giselle spat blood on the ground in a spray. She raised up on her knees, holding up a hand and shaking her head. "Please, I've had enough! No more, no more! Please!" Giselle begged. The wicked expression on Constance's face intensified. The sight of blood and pain aroused her. If she had a dick, it would have been hard.

The femme fatal slid her foot forward and leveled her hands. Suddenly, she sprang into the air and swung her foot around in a Round House Kick. *Crackkk!* Constance landed back on the surface and Giselle went slamming face first onto the graveled ground. She was out cold and snoring hard. Constance yanked a knife from her sleeve and straddled Giselle's back. She pulled her head back by her hair. Her gloved hand snaked around her neck and that's when it happened, Eureka went hysterical.

"Noooooo! Nooo!" Eureka sprung from the couch and ran over to the hundred inch flat screen, slapping her hand against it. Tears cascaded down her face. "You hurt her and I'll kill you, bitch! I'll rip your fucking heart out!"

All of the shouting brought Fear running into the living room with his .9mm. Both hands wrapped around the handle, he swung the black pistol around looking for someone to put a bullet through. Once he saw it was Eureka, he lowered his banger and stepped beside her, staring up at the TV screen.

On the screen, Constance's head shot up and that wicked expression emerged on her face again as she held the knife at the end of an unconscious Giselle's neck. Figuring she had Eureka's attention, she let the dope fiend's face fall back to the ground and approached the camera.

"You wanna save mommy dearest here? You have your home wrecking ass at the address at the bottom of that coffin. I'll wait for you to find it," she said. Fear frowned once he saw the coffin. He knew it was the one he'd buried his son's memory in. He turned the coffin over and carved at the bottom of it was an address he was very familiar with.

"The Spot!" Fear blurted to no one in particular.

Eureka's head snapped in his direction. "You know where this place is at?"

"Yeah," he nodded.

"Be there at 9 o'clock tonight," Constance continued. "A minute later and I'm slicing her jugular. Be prepared to fight 'til the death. No guns, no knives, you bring these," she held up her fists. "The winner walks away with   Fear's   heart."

"I'll be there, you can count on it!" Eureka shouted up at the screen. "You hearrr meee?" Spit flew from off her lips and clung to the screen.

"Oh, yeah, if you bring any ass besides your own, mommy's taking a permanent dirt nap." The femme fatal swore. "I'm out." She cut off the camera and the screen went   blue.

Eureka dashed out of the living room into the master bedroom. Fear went after her. He found her strapping up a bulletproof vest and sliding on Timberland boots, lacing them up tightly.

"Where are you going?" Fear's face balled up.

"Where do you think?" She tucked her Glock on her waist.

"I'm coming with you." He moved to grab his T-shirt but what she said stopped him.

"No. You heard what she said. Anyone besides me shows up and my mom is dead. I can't take that chance."

Fear exhaled and ran his hand down his face, nodding his understanding.

Eureka cupped her hands around his face and kissed him passionately before heading for the door. Reaching the door, she turned back around to Fear. She had something on her mind and he could tell. It was written all over her face. He raised an eyebrow and threw his head back.

"Do you think—o do you think I can take her?" she asked seriously.

He shot her a look and she read what was exactly on his mind. He didn't have to say a word to her. He knew just as she did that she couldn't beat Constance. She was out classed. It didn't matter though because she had too much pride and heart to walk away now. Not only that, she had to give it a shot for her mother's sake. If she was lucky, the odds would turn in her favor.

"Right." She turned around and made her exit.

Be it life or death, she was going to meet her destiny head on.

CHAPTER TWELVE
Later that night...

Crunch was kneeled down before his grandmother's dresser in front of a holy shrine made up of a portrait of white Jesus, a cluster of burning glass bottle candles and a crucifix that hung along the portrait. His head was tilted and his eyes were closed. His fingers were interlocked within each other as he whispered a silent prayer. He couldn't believe he was going to raise his gun on a man he had deemed his blood brother. He and Ronny had been tight since second grade. They were together every single day. You hardly ever saw one without the other. It was as if they were joined at the hip. Now all of that history would be thrown away because tonight they would draw iron, not to defend one another's lives but to take the other's.

Crunch crossed his name in the sign of the crucifix and rose to his feet, picking up his Kevlar bulletproof vest. He strapped the vest on and pulled a stocking cap over his frizzy cornrows. Afterwards, he slipped on a black sweatshirt over the body armor and picked up his gun from the dresser. He chambered one in the head of it and tucked it at the small of his back. Next, he dumped a pillow out of a pillowcase and pushed the bed aside with his foot until he unveiled the black iron door of an in floor safe. On his knees, he did the combination on the dial, waited to hear the *Click* and opened the door. Inside there was stacks and stacks of crinkled bills held together by beige rubber bands. He cleaned out the safe and put everything back in place. He then stuck a letter he had written inside of an envelope and licked it closed, flipping off the light switch as he left the   bedroom.

When he entered the living room he found his

grandmother lying on the couch snoring. The light was out so the blue illumination from the television set danced on her face. He stood there for a time watching her chest rise and fall as he caressed her saggy black mole infested cheek. A smirk formed on his lips thinking of how good she'd been to him. Having rescued him from the foster home and raised him like he'd come right out of her womb. He sat the pillowcase of money by the couch and tucked the envelope under her. After draping a blanket over her, he kissed her on the cheek and turned the TV off with the remote control before he left.

*****

Ronny stood in the dresser mirror strapping on a thin Kevlar bulletproof vest. While he was getting ready for his meeting with Crunch, Antoinette was sitting on the bed watching him. Her nervousness was written all over her face. God had been merciful when he let her man come home the first time, but he may not be so lenient this next go around. Every night he got up and left to prowl the streets for Malvo, was a night he could possibly not come walking back through the door. Tonight was much like all of the nights before and each time he got strapped up and armed with that hammer he was taking a risk.

"Baby, can't chu just let this go?" she asked timidly. "We can just pack our stuff and get from outta here. We still got money. We could just leave tonight and never   look   back."

"Come on now, stop that shit!" He caught an attitude, lines forming across his forehead. "I'm not gonna quit until I got that nigga Malvo's blood on my shoes and his body on this gun." He wagged his jet black .9mm

Beretta. "You hear me? He disrespected my lady, my prince, and my home. He's gotta go and I'ma send 'em on his way." He *Click Clacked* one in the chamber and tucked it in the small of his back.

He picked up his black sweatshirt from off of the bed and pulled it over his head. He looked himself over in the mirror as he straightened out his sweatshirt, making sure his bulletproof vest wasn't visible through the fabric. Satisfied, he turned around to Antoinette. She was staring down at her hands as she fidgeted with them. She was visibly trembling and she looked worried. He grabbed her by the wrist and pulled her up, wrapping his arms around her. Her arms wormed around his neck and she held him tightly. He could hear her sobbing as he caressed her back, kissing the side of her face and head. He loved her. When he was locked up in that homemade prison he thought about all of the side pussy he had been getting on her and felt horrible. He had a good thing at home and he had been taking a chance on losing it by banging outside chicks. *Damn*, he thought as he took a deep breath and inhaled the perfumed accenting her skin. He closed his eyes and brushed his cheek up against hers relishing in the moment. He always knew he'd loved her but man it didn't feel any realer than the moment they were sharing now. He pulled back and kissed her twice on the lips. She held his face cupped in her hands, staring into his eyes.

"Come back to me Ronny, come back to us," she spoke seriously. "Me and your son."

"I will, baby. Not even death will keep me away from my family, you hear me?" She looked down in doubt but hoping what he said would be the truth. With a curled finger, he tilted her chin up so she would be looking him directly in the eyes. "Antoinette, did you hear me?"

She timidly nodded *yes*.

"Hold up." She walked around him en route to the dresser. She opened her antique jewelry box which looked like it belonged to some English queen back in the 17th century. She opened the lid and fished through the earrings inside with her index and thumb until she uncovered what she was looking for. A smirk blessed her face as she pulled out a thin gold necklace with a unique charm. She motioned for him to give his back to her and he did. She then talked to him as she clamped the necklace around his neck.

"My great grandmother gave this to my great grandfather for good luck before he was sent off to war."

"Did it work?"

"He returned home with barely a scratch on him."

"And you believe it was because of this necklace?" he asked facing her, stroking the necklace with his hand while glancing down at it.

"I *know* it was because of the necklace," she said sincerely.

She turned him back around, kissing him on the lips and hugging him. She closed her eyes and took in his scent as the tears seeped from between her lids.

"Damn you, Ronny Montgomery, and damn me," she rasped.

"For what, baby?" he inquired, stroking her back lovingly.

"For falling in love with you."

"Damn, Malvo too, then." Ronny's face tightened as he bit down on the corner of his lip. "'Cause when I find 'em I'ma give 'em every shell this ratchet holds, that's on my momma."

*****

Ronny played the back of the Benz with Vladimir. He had the weight of the earth on his scrawny shoulders and it grew heavier the closer he got to his destination. As much as he tried to fight back the thoughts of what lay ahead, he couldn't. About five minutes from now, he'd be coming face to face with a childhood friend in an old fashion Western Showdown. The day the best friends dived headfirst into the game they knew there were two outcomes, death or prison. They'd already been on that iron vacation, and knew the longer they stayed down they'd most likely return to the cage or feel the interior of a coffin. In fact, they were both prepared for the inevitable. They knew that death was right around the corner. But neither of them thought he'd see that day on the account of the other.

Just thinking about having to kill his closest comrade brought tears to Ronny's eyes, but he'd be damned if he'd let them fall. Not after the way Crunch and Malvo had violated his lady and his son. The thoughts of wifey and his seed being tormented caused his forehead to crinkle and his nose scrunched. He was pissed off. *Fuck all of that shit,* he thought. *Bitch-ass nigga 'pose to be my people and he allowed this mothafucka to terrorize my home? Uh uh, he gotta go and this Beretta gone give him his boarding pass.* He held up the black pistol and admired it lovingly, before laying it back down in his lap and sucking on the end of the L.

"We're here." The chauffer announced over his shoulder.

With that said Ronny took a couple more tokes from the blunt and passed it to the Russian drug lord. He then said a quick prayer and crossed his heart in the name of   the   Lord.

"There's no need to worry, Ronny." Vladimir told him. "I've got eyes and guns everywhere." He motioned a finger around and told him where he had snipers hidden within the nearby warehouses. "They've been given strict orders to cut our friend down."

"Nah," Ronny shook his head. "He may have done me dirty, but me and that nigga out there got history. We were once brothers. I'ma play this one square. It's The Game of Death and only one of us will be walking away victorious."

Vladimir blew smoke out of his nose and mashed out the blunt in the ashtray. "You sure this is the way you wanna go about it?"

Ronny picked up the charm of his necklace from his chest. He held it pinched between his thumb and finger, before kissing it. He looked to the Russian and nodded, "Yeah."

"Alright, suit yourself."

Ronny climbed out of the back of the Benz prepared to meet his fate.

*****

Crunch pulled into the path between the two condemned warehouses and murdered the engine. He plucked the roach end of a blunt he'd been smoking earlier from out of the ashtray and stuck it between his thick blackened lips. As he cupped a hand around the roach and sparked it up, his eyes inadvertently wandering up to the rosary hanging from the rearview mirror. He watched as it swayed back and forth. He'd never been religious but he needed something other than a gun on his side if he hoped to walk away from this ordeal. After finishing off what was left of the L, he dropped the remnants into the ashtray. When he opened up the glove-box and reached for the bottle of Hennessy, he saw Ronny climbing out of the back of a Benz.

Crunch took a long guzzle from the bottle, he closed his eyes and hissed like a feral cat. If tonight was to be his last night alive, he wanted to be shit faced when he went out. He took one last quick guzzle, tossed the bottle on the front passenger seat and recovered his banger where he'd stashed it. Swinging open the door, he hopped out of the car and walked out in front of it. He and Ronny stood about fifteen feet from another. They both looked up into the black sky at the twinkling stars. The night was cool and calm with the occasional sound of speeding cars every now and again. A cool breeze brushed across the opposing men's faces, disturbing the loose hairs of Crunch's cornrows and Ronny's mustache. They relished in the moment and took deep breaths. They took in their surroundings because tonight could be either one of their last breathing.

Both men brought their heads down from looking up into the sky. Although Ronny was the first to peel his eyelids open, Crunch was the first to speak.

"So, this is what it's come to, huh? Two brothers in a duel to the death?" Crunch asked.

"You brought it to this Cane and Abel shit, so don't go blaming me, *brother*. You and that piece of shit invaded my home and violated my fucking family!" The meat of his brows formed together and he gritted his teeth, clutching his banger even tighter. "Tonight you answer for that with your corpse."

"Is that how you want it, my nigga?"

"That's how you made it." Ronny's eyes turned glassy as he sneered, the corner of his top lip twitching. "Malvo brainwashed us, had us doing his bidding. We were his puppets. Well, I'm not dancing on his strings anymore, I'm severing those ties."

"I did what I did. Am I sorry for it? Yes." Crunch spoke sincerely. "But I'm sure that won't change anything between us." He waited for his response.

"Right," Ronny replied. "Are you ready for yo tombstone, nigga?"

Crunch gripped his ratchet tighter causing his knuckles to crackle. In a blink of an eye the best friends' guns lifted and they charged after one another, exercising their   trigger-fingers. Their burners jerked inside of their palms and they spat perturbed, lighting up the night as their sneakers trampled the graveled ground.

Crunch! Crunch! Crunch!
Bloc! Bloc! Bloc! Bloc!
Boc! Boc! Boc! Boc!
"Ahhhhhh!"
"Ahhhhhh!"

A hot one skinned the side of Crunch's arm. Another one struck him just beneath the strap of his bulletproof vest, causing a red mist to filter the air. The charcoal black thug gritted his teeth and scowled, fighting back the fires in his body. He pressed on squeezing off on his opposition, two slugs smashed into Ronny. He scowled and gritted his teeth as well, stumbling a little but moving forth, letting that black thang go ham.

Boc! Boc! Boc!
Bloc! Bloc! Bloc! Bloc!

Ronny dropped down to a knee, keeping his balance by pressing his burner into the ground. He clenched his teeth as his throbbing chest slammed up against his Kevlar vest while he breathed heavily.

Crunch staggered toward his best friend, warm gun in his palm wafting with smoke. It was going to break his heart to do what he had to do but he had already opened that door, so he had to walk through it. One man made a sudden move that would cost him his life. The sounds of gunfire consumed the air. The other man's eyes snapped open and his bottom lip quivered as a sliver of blood ran, dripping upon his chest. He looked into the eyes of his executioner accusingly.

"You made me do this man, you! Not me!" The man doing the shooting claimed. He felt warm stinging in his eyes as they rimmed with tears. They sped down his cheeks as he held the other man close, one hand at the back of his neck and the other pressing his ratchet into his stomach. He took the gun from his abs and gently laid him on the ground. He sat his banger on the asphalt and gripped his hand with both of his. He lay on the surface with moist eyes and blood bubbling in his mouth.

Meanwhile inside of the Benz, Vladimir hung his head and shook it after seeing what had occurred.

"Gurgle. Gurgle. Gurgle." The blood trickled on both side of the fatally wounded man's head. The tears flowed from his eyes freely and his right leg twitched repeatedly. He could feel himself being pulled into the grave.

Lloyd Banks *Til The End* played in both of the men's heads, serenading the moment.

You look behind you when you turn the corna/Cause death is promised you seen some niggas go before ya and threats are honest and with that lingering in the back of ya head/ Ya know it's possible that you won't make back in ya bed/ The confusion of jealously and dishonor will spin ya/But there's nothing that hurt worse than when that gun powders in ya.

"What's wrong with chu, bro?" Crunch asked concerned, gripping a fourteen year old Ronny's shoulder.

"I just realized I'm out here by myself." Ronny's voice cracked as he wiped the tears that burst from his eyes. "A nigga ain't got no family, G."

"What chu mean? You brother is right here." He tapped his fist against his chest.

"Don't get me wrong, you my boy and all, but we're not blood." He told him as he wiped his face with the inside of his tank top.

"I can change that now."

A confused expression crossed Ronny's face. He didn't know what he could possibly do to change things.

"How?" he asked curiously.

"Easy." Crunch pulled a switch-blade from the back pocket of his Dickies. He triggered the blade and took Ronny's hand. He tried to yank it back but Crunch held fast.

"What chu doing?"

"Relax." Ronny took a deep breath and allowed his friend to do as he pleased. Crunch pricked his palm and he winced. When he looked down, a dot of blood had manifested. "Keep your hand out."

Crunch wiped the blade off on his pants leg and pricked his own palm, a dot of blood appeared. He closed the switch blade and shoved it in his back pocket. He extended his trickling hand toward Ronny. "Blood Brothers."

Ronny cracked a smir. "Blood Brothers," he said, gripping his hand. The pact was sealed in blood.

If you my nigga you my nigga 'til the end / Fuck a bill, fuck a bitch, fuck a Benz /Let's toast 'til we die/ Roll up the weed and blow the smoke in the sky/ If you my nigga you my nigga 'til we go /One of the few I would take a bullet fo/ Let's toast 'til we die/ Roll up the weed and blow the smoke in the sky

The fatally wounded man went still looking off to the side at nothing as he was held in the other man's arms. The surviving man's eyes twinkled as tears danced in them. His shoulders shook and his tears pelted his dead homie's face.

"I'm sorrrrryyyyy. Ahhh hahaha, I'm so sorrrrryyyyy." He sobbed and snot dripped from his nose as he rocked back and forth. "I didn't wanna do it! You made me, man! You made me, mannnaannn!" He closed his eyes and swallowed, pulling himself together. He wiped his face with his sleeve and leaned over, kissing his dead friend on the   forehead.

"I love you, brother, rest in paradise."

CHAPTER THIRTEEN

Hearing someone knock at the double doors of the building caused Constance to look alive from where she was sitting on the enormous pipe, Indian style with a black pipe in her grip. A satanic smile curled her lips and she pushed off of it, leaping down to the surface. Landing with the grace of a feline, she slowly stood erect. The building was so dark all she could make out was a short silhouette as it came through the door, moving in her direction. The double doors closed shut behind it.

"I knew that you'd come, even though you know you stand about a snow ball's chance in hell at beating me head up." Constance closed her eyes and shook her head, looking back up at her opponent. "That pride is a muthafucka, boy, and it's going to be the death of you." She threw down the pipe and it clanked against the floor. She then pulled off her jacket and tossed it aside. Eureka was still stalking forward, moving as if she didn't have a care in the world. Constance cracked the knuckles on both of her hands. "Alright, bitch, that's far enough." When Eureka kept coming, she snatched her .45 from the holster strapped to the small of her back and pointing it. "Fuck I tell yo' hard headed ass? You keep coming and I'ma bust yo onion wide open, you understand me?"

Suddenly she stopped, staring Constance dead in the eyes. For the first time the femme fatal saw her face since she'd emerged through the double doors. It wasn't Eureka at all. It was Fear. Constance's brow arched and her lips peeled back in a sneer. Her face twitched uncontrollably she was so mad.

"Where is she?" she grumbled, her head snapped around, trying to locate Eureka.

"She's not here. I came alone," Fear admitted. "She didn't listen. I told her if she didn't come, I'd slit her mother's throat."

"I'm here," Fear said. "That's all that matters. It's just me and you, like you always wanted."

Constance's forehead wrinkled and she narrowed her eyes. She tilted her head to the side as if she was studying him. "What's your angle?"

"There is no angle," he confessed. "I finally came to realize who I love the most. This whole time the love of my life was right under my nose and I hadn't even noticed her 'til now, foolish of me." He shook his head shamefully, slowly approaching with his hands up, palms showing. "I got rid of Eureka and Anton. You can come home now. We can sit down and talk. See where this thing goes." He spoke with a calm and steady voice.

Constance twisted her lips and tilted her head back up. "Fuck I look like, nigga? You telling a bitch all of the things she wanna hear, but I know it's some bullshit." She aimed the .45 right between his eyes, but he kept on coming. He was Fearless, so he wasn't afraid of anything. Not even death. "I'ma put a hot one right between your eyes."

"Go ahead then," Fear challenged her. "Kill the only man that has ever truly cared for you, blow my brains out," he stated with a soft voice. "You know how to do it. I taught you, one in the head and two in the sternum."

Constance's eyes filled with tears that came bursting free and streaming down her cheeks. Her bottom lip puffed out as she broke down crying. She still loved him. If she chose to lay him down, there wasn't any doubt in her mind that she'd take herself out right after. She'd put that thang under her chin and pull the trigger. Just like that.

"Put the gun down," he spoke again.

"Uh uh, no no," She shook her head rapidly and wiped her wet face with the back of her hand. She stayed planted exactly where she was with her banger extended right at his helmet. Her finger was putting pressure on the trigger, and the slightest squeeze would blast his brain through the back of his skull. At that moment his life was teetering between life and death, like it always did when he left the house vested and hammered up on a mission.

"Constance, put the gun down." He continued after her. His hands were still up. His eyes zeroed in on hers as he spoke peacefully. His voice soothed all of the hurt she felt   inside.

"Fuck you, Alvin!" she roared. Her eyes took on intenseness as she gritted her teeth. Images of Eureka jawing him in the bathroom played within her head like a matinee. She thought about the whipping he'd given her, his carving the tattoo off of her hand and banishing her from his home. Just when she was about to pull the trigger, he did the unthinkable. He spoke the words that made her heart   skip   a   beat.

"I love you," he spoke with a stern face. He said it with believability and his eyes were the polygraph. He was telling the truth. Those words wiped that hostile expression from Constance's face and all of their tender moments and good times went through her mental. The day he had saved her from the brothel and nursed her back to health, finding out she was pregnant and how joyous he was, comforting her inside of the hospital that night, all of the times they'd had sex. She wanted to believe him, she had to believe him, but most importantly, she needed to believe him.

"Tell me again." The tears slicked down her cheeks.

He stopped dead smack in front of her with the

barrel of her gun pressed into the meat between his eyes. He was still locked into her gaze. He was as serious as an Ebola outbreak. She watched his mouth. His lips slowly peeled apart and the words rolled off of his tongue like his name. She could feel their sincerity as they dripped from his   vocal   cords.

"I love you."

Those words were paralyzing to her. They choked her up. She stood there wide eyed with her mouth stuck open, holding her gun on him as she stared into his eyes, trying to read any signs of fuckery that may lie hidden within them. He was keeping that shit one hundred with her. She could feel it at her core. She'd waited for so long to hear those words and know for a fact they were true. Constance's face slightly jumped as she stood in a pause with her banger pressed against her mentor's forehead. She closed her eyes and a fresh set of tears coated her face, dripping off of her chin and splashing on her Timberland boots. She took a deep breath and peeled her eyes back open. Her eyes settled back on Fear's as she rasped out of breath. What he had said knocked the wind out of her lungs.

Slowly, Fear grasped her wrist and lowered the gun from his forehead. Using his other hand, he pulled the weapon from her hand and tucked it at the small of his back. He cupped her face and stared deeply into her eyes. She could see the emotions swimming inside of his pupils. At long last she could finally feel what she'd always wanted from him. Love. That real shit that was oh so special. Some had felt it, and those who did had been lucky, extremely lucky. Now it was her turn. All she needed now was a kiss for the confirmation that his love was as genuine as she believed it was.

Fear opened his mouth and his bottom lip swept up against Constance's. He slipped her a little tongue as he kissed her softly, gently, tenderly and then deeply, giving her just a smidgen more of tongue. He rotated his head slightly to the left as their mouths molested each other. Their breathing grew heavier. Fear slid his fingers in between her dread locks, intertwining them. Her hands settled on his waist as they made out. He pulled his head back and her eyes slowly opened, looking up at him. A smirk formed on her lips. She looked like she was intoxicated. She was. She was drunk in love. It felt like a century had passed as he stood their locked in her hazel brown eyes, caressing her cheeks with his thumbs. Then suddenly, out of the blue, a sound occurred that broke the silence.

Snappp!

Constance's neck sounded like a chicken bone being broken in half. She fell limp, but he caught her before she could meet the ground. He slowly lowered her to the surface. She looked at peace in his arms as if she was just taking a nap, but there wasn't any doubt that she was dead. The killer combed his fingers through his protégé's dread locks as he stared down into her face, tears pooling in his eyes.

He opened his mouth. "Constance." His voice crackled with sorrow as he lay his forehead against hers, staining her cheeks with his tears. His shoulders shook as he sobbed, hating himself for having to kill her. She was as much a part of his life as he was hers. He could count on both hands how many times she'd pulled his ass out of a tight squeeze and showed him what it was like to be loved unconditionally. Before he didn't think such a thing even existed but she'd proven to him that it did. Even after murdering the love of his life, he still held a special place in his heart for her.

Fear picked his head back up and wiped the tears that emitted from his eyes. He looked back down into the face of his first student. "...Constance, I hope you find the love in death that I could not give you in life." He kissed her tenderly on the lips and then on the forehead, gently stroking the side of her face. Hearing someone coming through the double doors at his rear, he drew the .45 and pointed it. A moment later Eureka emerged. She cautiously approached looking all around the building before her eyes took notice of Fear on the ground with Constance in his arms. She looked from his tear streaked face to her limp body.

"Is she?" she asked.

"Dead," he replied.

She gave him a resentful expression. He picked up immediately on what she was getting at.

"There wasn't any way you could have beaten her, Reka." Fear gave her the truth. "I trained Constance myself. I taught her everything she knew. With her experience and skills, she would have made short work of you I'm sorry but that's the truth."

Eureka nodded in understanding. He was right. There wasn't any chance of her beating his protégé in a head up match. Constance had fought and murdered more people than he cared to remember. She was proficient with just about every weapon. And even without something in her hands she still wasn't someone to take lightly. With her fighting skills she was as deadly as she was with two guns in her hands. Fuck Mel Gibson, she was the *real* Lethal Weapon.

"Oh, shit!" Eureka's eyes widen and her jaw dropped. She took off running right past Fear and into the corridor. She moved down the hallway looking all around as she made hurried steps, calling her mother's name. Hearing growling ahead, she froze where she was and took a gander. She looked closely and tried to peer through the darkness. Just then the Rottweiler's stepped forth, heads tilted as they stared down Eureka trying to intimidate her. Their lips twitched and showcased their canines as they slowly stepped forth, one paw at a time.

Eureka took a step back and reached for the gat on her hip. She was about to get busy with that thang until a voice boomed at her back.

"Terror. Evil. Stand down." Fear's voice echoed off of the walls. At his command the hounds sat on their hind legs panting and looking as harmless as toothless Vipers. Fear kneeled to the dogs rubbing their shiny coats as they licked his palms and face. "I miss y'all too, it's been a while." Growing tired of playing with the pooches, he said, "Alright, that's enough. Y'all leave Daddy alone and go play." With the order delivered, Evil and Terror traveled down the hall playing with one another. Fear stood up and snatched his .9mm from the holster on his hip. He now hand two bangers in his hands.

"Eureka! Is that you, baby girl?" Eureka heard Giselle deep within the bowels of the building.

"Mommy, keep talking so I can find you!" Eureka hollered out.

"I'm down here!"

"Alright, I'm coming!" Eureka tapped Fear and they hurried down the corridor, listening to her mother call her name time and time again. Her voice brought them to a thick iron door with a filthy window. Eureka peered through it and saw her mother shackled to a floor to ceiling pipe. She grabbed the door handle, turned it and pushed her shoulder up against the door. The iron door cried aloud as it was pushed inward. Eureka ran over to her mother and hugged her, happy to see her alive. She looked into her face and she looked like she'd been used as a punching bag. Her face was wet with blood and perspiration. Both of her eyes were almost swollen shut and her lips were plump from the thorough ass whopping Constance put on her. Giselle cracked a smile and she made out the two missing teeth on the side of her mouth. Seeing how her mother had been unkept, done pissed Eureka off. She wished she could bring Constance back to life and fade her ass herself.

"Damn, ma, how you holding up?" Eureka winced as she looked her mother's wounds over. Constance had done a real number on her.

"I'll be fine, baby girl." She whispered in a hoarse voice, barely conscious. "I just need to—" Suddenly her eyes bulged and her lips peeled apart as she stared up at something terrifying. Eureka's brows furrowed. She snatched her Glock off of her waist and whipped around. Fear kicked the gun out of her hands and it skidded across the floor, spinning in circles. He then pointed his .9mm at Giselle's dome piece and the .45 at Eureka.

"Move out of the way, Reka," he spat heatedly. His face masked by hatred. He was on fire.

"Fear, no, she's my mother." Eureka reasoned.

"Fuck that 'pose to mean to me?" Fear grumbled. "This dope fiend took me for everything I had. It's gone, now she gotta go with it. Peace out!" He went to pull the trigger and she shielded her mother, looking over her shoulder at him with pleading eyes that threatened to spill tears. He was hot and his blood was boiling like a pot of water on the stove. The killer in him screamed for blood, not mercy. He squeezed the handle of his ratchet so tightly he could feel it making an imprint in his palm. His finger twitched on the trigger, anxious to feel the recoil of the gun when it was fired. The slightest brush of his index would send Giselle to a place with bright lights, plenty of clouds and winged people. Just when he made up his mind to stroke the trigger, Eureka's pleading eyes zapped all of the hatred out of him. His face softened seeing her at his mercy. He didn't know what it was about her that made him so weak. It was the same thing that Italia did to him when he saw her in pain. All he wanted to do was take her into his arms and let her know everything would be okay.

He'd told Constance that a killer with a heart didn't have longevity in this game, and now here he was crippled by the same emotions he'd chastised her for. *This fucking heart of mines,* he thought, lowering his bangers to his sides.

Eureka closed her eye for a moment and took a deep breath, thankful that the assassin had shown mercy. As soon as she opened them she found him lifting one of the guns again but before she could protest any further he'd already hugged the trigger.

Poc! Zing!

A molting bullet broke the handcuff at the bracelet, setting Giselle free. Fear lowered the smoking .45 and stared down at the dope fiend with animosity. She was able to make out his malevolent eyes from the bluish illumination shining through the gated window. The look he was giving her was enough to make even the hardest of cats   kill   over   on   the   spot.

"I'm going to bury Constance's body," he said with

his eyes glued on Giselle, making her feel uncomfortable under his gaze.

"I'm going to take my mother to the hospital. I'll meet you back at the house."

Fear eyes stayed on her mother for a while before he spoke his final peace, "Alright." He headed out of the boiler room with the Rottweilers following behind him, tails wagging. Once he was gone, Giselle sighed with relief.

*****

The cave was dark and wet. It was quiet save for the sound of droplets of water hitting the small puddles scattered throughout the surface. Just at the opening a silhouette carrying something moved about hastily until it was engulf by the darkness. There was shuffling then the clinking of metal, then a flame was born. Its illumination shone on Fear's face. He used its light as a guide to see where he was going. He readjusted the strap of the bag on his shoulder and unzipped the worn black leather duffle bag. He withdrew a stick wrapped in torn rags and deposited it into an opening in the wall. He soaked it with a tin can of lighter fluid and brought the flame forth. *Frooosh.* The stick went up so fast he jumped back before it could scorch his face. The burning fire of the torch wafted at the air.

Fear went along the walls of the cave depositing identical sticks and lighting them up until the cave was nicely lit. Once he was done, he slipped the Zippo lighter into his jeans and feasted his eyes on the site before him. It was a nest of branches with a thick blanket of genuine lambs' wool. The killer jogged out of the cave past Constance's body, which lay covered by a sheet. When he returned, he had a husky suitcase. He set it on the ground and opened it. Inside there were several items.

He drew the sheet from his protégé's prone body and tossed it aside. Constance lay giving the appearance she was asleep. She was draped in all black. She wore an army jacket, cargo pants and Timberland boots. This was what she donned every time she and Fear went out on a mission.

Fear picked her up and laid her inside of the nest upon the lambs' wool. He stuck her .45 in her hand and laid it down at her waist. He then began placing items inside of the nest beside her: a shotgun, a box of shells, a bowie knife, flashlight, and a portrait of them out at dinner, another one of her, her mother, father and sister. This was how the Vikings were buried some time ago. Their loved ones placed them in nests, buried them in the ground and laid them on boats that would be set on fire. The Vikings were buried with items they cherished along with their weapons. The weapons were in case they ran into any trouble on their journey into the afterlife.

Constance had told Fear she wanted her funeral to be just like theirs were. They were warriors, and so was she.

Fear pulled one of the torches out of the wall and engaged the female assassin's still form. Holding the torch above his head, he caressed her forehead as he stared down into her face. He couldn't get over how at peace she looked then. She had been through a hard life and finally she'd get her chance to rest in paradise. Thinking of this brought a grin to his face as his thumb swept up and forehead, lovingly.

"Have a safe trip, ma." He kissed her forehead. He then walked around the nest, touching the torch to it and igniting it. He tossed the torch aside and walked toward the mouth of the cave. Once he got to the end of it, he stopped and turned around. He watched the flames as they devoured the nest and Constance's body. He closed his eyes and said a silent prayer before disappearing.

Tranay Adams

CHAPTER FOURTEEN
five hours later...

When Fear came through the door he found Eureka and Anton sitting at the kitchen table. He took off his trench coat and hung it on the coat stand.

"You took care of that?" Eureka asked.

"Yeah," he nodded. "Your mother?"

"I took her to the hospital. She'll walk with a limp the rest of her life and her hand is permanently disfigured but she'll be all right."

"Where is she?"

"She's upstairs asleep. Those pain killers knocked her out."

Fear nodded and looked to Anton. "What's up, baby boy? How's that leg?"

"It's alright," he replied with a jaw full of his sandwich.

"Well, I don't know about y'all but after the day I've had, I need a drink." She excused herself from the table and headed down into the basement.

"Damn, youngin' you ain't showing that sub no love."

"I'm hungry as shit, man," he replied, steadily munching. He then picked up a glass of juice and washed his food down.

"You want me to hit chu?" Fear asked.

Anton nodded *yes*.

Fear grabbed the glass and a carton of Minute Maid fruit punch from out of the refrigerator. He turned his back as he sat the glass on the counter, pouring it full before closing the carton.

Anton chewed down his food and wiped his mouth. Seeing Fear approaching from his right, he turned to take the glass of juice. He drunk it down and sat it back on the table, belching. He then lay back in the chair with hooded eyes and his head bobbling about lazily.

"Damn, that lil' bit of food got me with the itis." He claimed. "I'm sleepy than a mothafucka, boy."

Fear stood at the sink wearing a stone face watching his protégé. Anton's vision became blurred and his image of his mentor separated, moving to and from one another. He blinked his eyes hurriedly and tilted his head down as he was trying to get a better look at him from a different angel. Sluggishly, he rose to feet and hobbled toward the killer on one leg, eventually falling to the floor.

"Ooof," He hit the linoleum grimacing and looking up.

"What the—what the fuck—did you put in my drink, nigga?"

Fear didn't say a word. He watched as Anton made several failed attempts to get back upon his feet. But eventually the drug he'd laced his drink with took its full effects and his face slammed into the floor.

Fear pulled an envelope from his back pocket as he kneeled down to Anton. He tucked the envelope into his pocket and brushed a hand over his head, before kissing his temple. Hearing noise that sounded like something sliding up into the ceiling, his head shot up and he moved to head down stairs into the basement.

*****

Eureka poured herself a shot and threw it back. She poured up another shot and was about to down that one as well when something stole her interest. Her eyes darted to their corners to the section of the wall she saw Fear knock on days prior. She threw back the shot and sat the glass down on the bar top. She approached the wall and molested it with both hands as she moved along it. Stopping at a space she pressed her ear against it and knocked. *Bingo*, she thought, hearing the hollow sound in it. She then knocked on the space in the same pattern and rhythm as she saw Fear do. The wall shot up, startling her and causing her to stagger back. She narrowed her eyes and tried to peer through the darkness inside of the secret room. She approached with caution, taking calculated steps as she crossed the threshold.

Eureka pulled the drawstring of the light bulb dangling at the center of the room and bathed the space in light. Bringing her arm down, she looked about taking in the room. One wall was full of weapons ranging from handguns, assault rifles, knives and grenades. The other wall was aligned with costumes, masks, and wigs. The getup that really stood out was the wig of thick long dreadlocks and a trench coat. Eureka was in awe looking from wall to wall. She looked up at the wall ahead and what she saw made her sick to her stomach and weak in her knees. The wall was loaded with the black and white photographs of people she'd never seen before but she was sure were targeted to be killed for whatever reason. Very visible amongst the photographs was a picture of Bootsy, Giselle and a younger Eureka and Anton. Her father's face was circled in a red marker. Below the pictures, on a desk top, was her father's gold name bracelet. She couldn't believe it. The whole time her father's killer had been right under her nose, she had been sleeping with him.

Tears quickly flooded her face drenching it wet.

She placed her quivering hands over her mouth and staggered back like she'd been shot. She began sobbing hard but stopped once she backed into what felt like a statue. She spun around swiftly and locked eyes with her father's murderer, Fear. One hand over her mouth, she staggered back looking up at him like he was the spawn of Satan in all of his glory: long black horns, bat wings, clutching a pitchfork with flames dancing all around him. He looked upon her wearing a sorrowful face not knowing what to say to her exactly. All he knew was his secret had devastated her and that things could never go back to how they were between them.

"Eureka, I…"

"You killed him?" Her voice cracked emotionally. "You killed my daddy."

He hung his head and took a deep breath, slumping his shoulders. He then looked back up at her and nodded, his eyes were full of guilt. His thoughts took him back to that faithful night like a time machine.

It was just after midnight when Bootsy got off of his twelve hour shift at the warehouse. Stepping out onto the sidewalk, he lit up a cigarette and waved goodbye to his coworkers before he fell in step toward the parking lot where his car was parked. Being it was Friday and the end of the work week, the fellas had decided to go out for a couple of cold ones at the bar up the block. They'd tried to get him to come along. He weighed it and the moment he did his aching back and feet made him reconsider. Bootsy took a rain check and decided to head home to a nice hot bath and a comfortable bed. Just thinking about his cozy mattress made him sleepy and brought a smile to his face.

He imagined himself snuggled under those thick blankets with his head nestled against a fluffy pillow.

"Man, I can't wait to see my bed," he said aloud to no one in particular, taking a drag from his square and allowing the smoke to filter his lungs. Coming upon his Toyota Corolla, he switched hands with the cigarette and fished around inside of his pocket for his car keys. He unlocked the door and hopped in behind the wheel. He turned the key in the ignition and the dashboard lit but the engine didn't start. Folds ran across his forehead as he wondered what the fuck was up. "Aww, come on, not tonight." He turned the key twice more and nothing still didn't happen. "Oh, fuck you, fuck you!" He hurled insults up at Lord Almighty as he stared up at the ceiling. He snatched the Joe out of his mouth and said, "Haven't I've gone through enough over the fucking years, huh? Gimmie a break, will ya?" He punched the ceiling once and tried to start the car again. Realizing she wasn't going to crank up, he popped the hood and hopped out of the car. He pissed and moaned about all of his rotten luck and how his day had been dampened by bullshit as he stepped to the front of the car. He lifted the hood up and propped it up with the rod. Taking his square into his mouth, he pulled out his cell phone and used the blue glow its screen illuminated to see what was wrong with it internally. Once he couldn't find anything wrong, he decided to shift a couple of wires around to see if that would get it running again.

"You need any help?" A masculine voice rang out of the night startling Bootsy.

Thunk! He threw his head up fast and it slammed against the hood. Wincing, he looked from where the voice came, rubbing the back of his head. Standing a couple of feet away was a man in a hoodie with dreadlocks spilling from out of it. He narrowed his eyes trying to get a good look at his face but the night partially hid it.

"Sorry about that. I didn't mean to startle you."

"It's alright." He made out the sky blue button down shirt he was wearing that had Pep Boys stitched on one side of it. "Pep Boys, huh?"

"Yeah, I'm just leaving a friend of mines house, heading to the bus stop," he said. "I saw you over here and thought I could help out."

"Thanks. I appreciate that. Uh…"

"Oh, I'm sorry. I'm Tony," he extended her hand.

He shook his hand. "Bootsy."

"Nice to meet cha. It's Boosty like Collins, right? The singer?"

"Yep," he nodded with a smirk.

"Mind if I take a look at it?" He motioned toward the hood of the car with his hand.

"Oh, sure, go right ahead." He moved out of his way. While he got busy under the hood, he got back inside of the vehicle behind the wheel, ready to turn the key when he told him to.

Tony plucked the small flashlight from out of his shirt's pocket and used its light to check things out. "There you are. The little fella that's been giving my buddy, Boosty, here a hard time." He stuck the flashlight into his mouth and used both hands to rectify the problem. Finishing, he stood erect. "Okay, Bootsy, try it now."

Bootsy did as ordered and the Nissan roared back to life. A smile stretched across his face and he clapped his hands. Tony let the hood down and approached his window looking at his oil smudged hands. He hunched down into the window. "Aye, you got anything in there I can wipe my hands with?"

"Yeah. I should have something, " he stated jovially, opening the glove box. "Thanks. I really appreciate this."

"Don't mention it. We're both black, we've gotta look out for our own."

Bootsy grabbed a handful of napkins out of the glove box and slammed it closed. As soon as he turned around he met the silencer of a black gun as it expelled hushed bullets.

Choot! Choot!

Bootsy's eyes snapped open and his mouth widen. He looked down at the holes in his chest running red streams and then back up into the eyes of his killer. Gasp! Gasp! Gasp! He tried to breathe as best he could, a trembling hand reaching out as tears ran from the corners of his eyes. Tony grabbed his hand and held it firmly. He gripped the silenced pistol as he stared dead into his wide eyes.

Gasp! Gasp! Gasp! Gasp!

"Shhh, it's okay, don't fight it. Just let it go. It will all be over in a second."

Bootsy peered out of narrowed lids, his eyes moving around lazily. His breathing grew fainter the more air he tried to draw into his lungs. His harsh wheezing and gasping made him sound like he was having an asthma attack. His grip had begun to loosen around the killer's hand and he was feeling faint.

"Attaboy, just let it go, nice and easy." Tony coached him. "You'll be at peace soon."

A moment later, Bootsy's head settled against the headrest and he stared off into space, releasing his last breath. Still holding his hand, Tony glanced at his watch and stood up. He opened the driver's door and turned the car off. After sifting through his pockets and relieving him of whatever money he had on him, he took the thick braided name bracelet from around his wrist. He crammed all of the items inside of his pocket and pulled his mangled brown leather wallet from his back pocket. He tucked it into his back pocket and closed the door back quietly. Standing erect, he crossed his heart in the holy crucifix and walked off with hands in his hoodie like he just didn't leave a nigga slumped in his whip.

Tony slid into the passenger seat of a silver Ford Mustang and slammed the door shut. As his accomplice pulled off, he pulled the gold name bracelet from his pocket and his worn leather wallet. He cracked the wallet open and snatched out the crisp dead presidents inside. Looking through the rest of the wallet he discovered a picture of Bootsy and his family. On the photograph there was a drug free Giselle, and a young Eureka and Anton. He studied the picture for a minute before tossing the tattered wallet out of the window.

"Who's that?" Constance stole a glance at the picture.

"The cat's family I just pushed to the other side." Fear tucked the photograph into his pocket and held up the name bracelet. 'Bootsy' was sitting on black onyx and outlined in gold. He traced the letters with his finger before stashing it inside of his hoodie's pocket.

*****

"But why?" Eureka croaked and swallowed the ball of hurt that formed in her throat. Fresh tears coated her face and she licked her lips, tasting the saltiness of them. "Why did you kill my daddy?"

Fear snatched the tranquilizer gun from the Velcro strapped holster on his thigh. Eureka zeroed in on it and then looked back up into his face. He told her exactly why he'd killed Bootsy. The truth was like a dagger through the heart. Her eyes became as big as pool balls and her mouth formed an O. She tried to say something but a cache of emotions had a strangle hold on her.

"I'm sorry, Reka." Fear lifted the tranquilizer gun and squeezed the trigger twice, it bucked. *Peewk! Peewk!* One dart stuck to her chest and the other off to the side above it. She felt her eyelids become heavy and her mouth fell open. She went to collapse but before she could he tucked the tranquilizer gun into its holster and scooped her up into his arms. He carried her out of the secret room, hind kicking the wall when he came out which closed the sliding wall shut. He laid her down on the couch and retrieved a roll of duct tape. He wrapped her mouth with it as well as bounded her wrists. With that done, he sat the duct tape down and ran his hand through her short curly hair, admiring her angelic face. He kissed her tenderly on the forehead and scooped her back up again, carrying her limp body up the staircase.

Fear deposited Eureka inside of the trunk and slammed it shut. When he hopped behind the wheel and peeled off. All he could think about was how he had stabbed her in the back.

Tranay Adams

CHAPTER FIFTEEN

Hearing muffled voices and shuffling at the trunk, Eureka squirmed around trying to work her wrists free from their bondages. Realizing her efforts were futile, she grew still. Right after the trunk was lifted open, a blinding light illuminated, stinging her eyes. She narrowed her eyes and turned her head away from the bright illumination. A familiar chuckling brought her head back around. She peered closely and when she made out the face staring down at her, *her* heart dropped. She was wide eyed at first but then her eyebrows arched and formed a scowl.

"My, oh my, aren't you a sight for sore eyes?" Malvo smiled wickedly and blew out smoke. He dropped his cigarette on the ground and mashed it out under his Timberland boot. He then grabbed her by the bondages of her wrists and dragged her out of the trunk, letting her hit the ground hard on her side.

"Ooof!"

She winced as the wind was knocked out of her. She lay still as she was drug across the ground. While this was happening she looked around taking in all of her surroundings. From what she could make out in the scarcely lit space she was inside of an old warehouse. Before she knew it she was being hoisted up from the ground and planted into an iron chair. She mad dogged Malvo as he took a step back, rubbing his hands as sinister plans formulated inside of his thinking cap. He had a thousand ways he wanted to torture her.

Eureka took in the hefty man that had been her headache those past couple of years. She noticed the rags wrapped around his wounds and the red dots that were expanding on them. He was bleeding badly but he was so focused on bringing her misery he didn't even seem to notice.

"Oh, how the tables have turned!"

Crack!

A hard right whipped Eureka's head around and she slumped. Her head came up lazily and she looked up through dazed eyes. She watched as Malvo popped the hatch of his truck and grabbed a black leather bag that looked like a bowling ball would be carried inside of. He closed the hatch and dropped the bag on the bootleg table that he had made himself out of an old wooden door and two empty trash cans. With that done, he stripped down to his wife beater and sifted through the bag until he found what he was looking for. A big Kool-Aid smile stretched across his face.

"Hold up!" Fear said, prompting him to turn around. "Let me at least say goodbye."

"Go right ahead."

Eureka glared at Fear as he advanced in her direction. She was so hot she could actually feel her body warming. The killer adjusted his trench coat and switched hands with the duffle bag. "I guess you're on one right now, huh? Here a nigga comes into yo life, makes you fall in love with 'em, then turns around and drives a mothafucking stake through yo heart. That's some cold shit, right?" Tears bled from her eyes as she mad dogged him. She clenched her jaws so tightly they throbbed. "Awww, don't cry, beautiful." He tried to caress the side of her face and she snapped her head away from him. "Listen, if it makes you feel any better, it was all business, nothing personal." He grabbed her by her bottom jaw and kissed her on the side of the face, resting the side of his head against hers for a time. When he stood back up, he looked at his watch. "Well, look at the time, I better get going." He moved past Malvo and patted him on the back as he headed for the exit.

Old sucker ass nigga, Malvo shook his head thinking of how he'd passed those counterfeit bills off to Fear. He then looked up at Eureka who was glaring at him intensely with veins running through her forehead. *Boy, oh boy, this little bitch is on fireeeee.* He blinked his eyes as he was becoming woozy but maintained keeping himself upon his feet. It had been some time since he'd been shot. And he was sweating and feeling feverish. He looked down and saw several small splatters of red that looked like ketchup.

"Shit, I better hurry up." He stole a look at his blood on the ground. He walked upon Eureka and pulled the collar of her shirt down over her right shoulder. He licked his lips and gripped the machete with both hands, hoisting it above his head. His sights were set on the point of her shoulder. He'd planned on slicing it off with one swing of the razor-sharp blade. "Now hold still, this only gonna sting a little."

Eureka closed her eyes tightly and clenched her jaws as she bowed her head, bracing herself for a marring. Malvo could feel his dick grow semi erect seeing the petrified look on her face. Her fear of the impending danger made him aroused, even his nipples had grown hard.

Sniktttt!

Eureka's hand went up the side of Malvo's face. His eyes bugged and his mouth snapped open. He felt heat and a searing pain on the left side of his head. He dropped the machete to the ground and grabbed for his ear, his hand came away slick with blood. When he looked down he found his severed ear on the ground beside his knee. He picked it up and pressed it to the side of his face and it fell again. Eureka tucked the box cutter Fear had slipped her and picked up the machete Malvo had dropped. As soon as he'd saw her going for it he scrambled to get away on his hands and knees.

She followed him whistling as she went along, admiring the sharpness of the blade and patting it into her palm. Seeing her prey getting away, she ran over and kicked him in the ass. His forehead slammed up against the ground, scraping the skin off of it. He pulled his face up grimacing, continuing his useless attempt at escaping.

Eureka walked over to the side of Malvo and kicked him in the temple. The impact tossed him on his back and left him staring up at the ceiling in a daze. His eyes moved around lazily in his head as he groaned. She straddled him and lifted his shirt exposing his hairy, flabby upper body. She smacked his left peck where his heart was and used the machete to carve a circle where she believed it was located. He winced feeling the sharp blade slit his skin causing blood to run. He struggled to get her off of him but he wasn't strong enough; his wounds had left him weak.

Eureka flipped the machete over in her palm and took it by both hands.

"You always were a heartless bastard, spiritually," she said, licking her lips as she held the machete above her head. "Now I'm gonna make it physically."

She moved to perform surgery and...

Boom!

The warehouse's door broke from its hinges and came crashing down on the ground. Siska and Ponytail came spilling through the door. Eureka's head snapped up seeing the men approaching. She pulled Malvo up onto his knees and pressed the machete against his throat, causing blood   to   trickle.

"Come any closer and I'm taking this nigga's head off on some Mexican cartel shit, on mommas." Eureka swore with a pair of menacing eyes. She believed that the Greeks had come to rescue Malvo from her.

"Easy there sweetheart, we don't want chu." Siska assured, stepping forward with his cane and flanked by his henchmen. "We want him—alive!"

"Oh, fuck!" Malvo's eyes took in the sight of Siska and his henchman.

Ponytail winked and blew him a kiss. He couldn't wait to get his hands on him.

"I give you him and I walk?" Eureka tried to get shit understood.

"Exactly," Siska nodded.

"How do I know this isn't a trick?"

"You don't know. But I can promise you that if you don't let us have him now, my man here is going to lay the both of you down and be done with it." Ponytail pointed both of his handguns with the extended magazines at Eureka and Malvo. "It makes me no difference. The choice is all yours, my dear."

"Hold it!" A voice rang from everyone's rear. When they looked, Vladimir, Ronny and the henchmen had their weapons drawn on them.

"No one make a move, the fat man's coming with us!" Ronny stated from behind the barrel of his shotgun.

"What the hell is going on here?" Eureka's face scrunched up as she wondered why Ronny had turned on Malvo.

"The fuck he is!" Ponytail turned his twin handguns on the hostiles.

"This man is in debt to us." Vladimir told Siska. "We've come to collect."

"I as well," Siska let him know. "He killed my nephew."

"He owes me a little over $700,000 dollars." Vladimir replied, looking over the length of his M-16 which was pointed dead at the old Greek.

"This dirty mothafucka got me tortured, raped my lady, and has probably left my son scarred for life." Ronny spoke up for his piece of the action. "I can't let 'em walk outta here with y'all."

"*We* can't let 'em walk out of here with him!" Vladimir corrected him.

The Greeks and the Russians locked into intense gazes, all of them hearing their hearts beating inside of their ears. At any giving moment triggers would be squeezed, guns would blaze and lives would be lost. All it would take was any of the opposing bosses' orders.

Eureka and Malvo stood off to the side watching the drama unfold.

"Gimmie the word, Siska, and I'll set it off." Ponytail talked out of the side of his mouth but kept his guns and his eyes on the threat before him.

"Stay ready." Siska spoke in a hushed tone.

"Just say it, boss, and we'll lay them both down." Nicolay had his assault rifle on Ponytail and was dying to light his ass up.

Vladimir didn't reply. He was willing to get into some gangsta shit but he was hoping the old man would fold seeing as how he was out gunned.

"May I make a suggestion?" Siska asked, breaking the tension.

"I'm listening," Vladimir stated.

Eureka and Malvo watched as the bosses engaged in conversation. They spoke in hushed tones so they couldn't make out anything that was said. Whatever was discussed they must have came to an agreement because both sides lowered their weapons. They then started in their direction.

"You're free to go," Siska spoke to Eureka. "Beat it, kid."

"Do I have your word that if I let him go you won't gun me down?" she inquired.

The old Greek gangsta lifted a hand. "I swear on my nephew's grave."

Eureka exhaled, took the machete from Malvo's throat, and backed her way up toward the door, keeping her eyes on everyone. Once she reached the exit, she dropped the machete and took off running.

*****

Nicolay and Mikhail held Malvo under each of his arms as they drug him toward a black Mercedes Benz. He was losing a lot of blood, dripping it everywhere.

As Siska and ponytail approached their Lincoln Town Car, the driver side door opened and the Amazon hopped out. She walked over to the back passenger door and opened it. Faith stepped out holding Heaven in her arms, they both were crying. Seeing Malvo being dragged away, they ran over to him. Faith dropped to her knees and hugged his neck while Heaven embraced his body. They both sobbed and kissed on his blood stained face. He came to slightly once he saw his wife and kid before his eyes.

"Baby," he said groggily, looking from his wife to his daughter. "Heaven is that you?"

"Yes, Daddy, it's me," Heaven cried. "Me and mommy."

"Oh, baby, we missed you so much." Faith hugged him tighter, kissing his lips and the side of his face. "What have they done to you?"

"It's —It's okay, honey, I'll be alright," Malvo lied. He knew that this would be the last time he'd see his most favorite girls in the world. "I thought—I thought you were dead."

"No baby, no," Faith shook her head as she swiped away her tears. "They murdered my parents, my sister and her best friend."

"Alright, move outta the way." One of the Russian henchmen ordered, pointing his M-16 at Faith.

Seeing the assault rifle scared the hell out of Heaven and she clung to her father screaming. "Shhhh, it's okay, baby girl," Malvo tried to calm her down. "Everything will be fine."

"No, daddy, no, they're gonna take you away from us."

"Get that kid and get the fuck outta here now!" The henchman spat. Malvo shot daggers at him and twisted his lips, wishing he could put something hot in his bitch ass for coming at his lady like that.

"Faith, take lil' momma and get outta here, get outta here now!" Malvo ordered.

"Noooooooo, let me goooooo!" Heaven screamed, tears streaming down her face as her mother pried her from her father.

The little girl wrapped her arms and legs around her mother tightly and buried her wet face into her bosoms, weeping. Faith kneeled down to Malvo. She held the side of his face and told him that she loved him.

"I love you too, baby. And I'm sorry, I'm sorry about all of this shit," he said sorrowfully, meaning every word of it.

Faith kissed her husband like it would be for the last time. In her heart she knew it was more than likely true. After allowing Malvo to kiss their daughter's head, she took off running as fast as she could. She got about twenty feet away before she turned around. She held her man's gaze one last time before making a mad dash from off of the warehouse's grounds.

With his wife and kid gone, the Russian's placed him into the backseat of the Mercedes Benz. One climbed in on each side of him and they slammed the doors shut.

"I'm glad that we could come to this agreement." Vladimir shook Siska's hand through the back passenger window of the Town Car.

"Me too," Siska stated. "You just be sure to call me when its time."

"You've got my word." Vladimir looked him dead in his eyes. A man's word was valued more than the American dollar when it was between men of honor. Every real nigga knew this but sadly that breed of men had grown to be an endangered species.

Siska nodded and the black tinted window closed. The Lincoln drove off of the grounds of the warehouse with Vladimir watching it. Once the red backlights of the car disappeared into the night, he made his way over to his own car and hopped into the backseat. The vehicle resurrected and pulled off, followed by several Mercedes Benzes.

"Are you alright?" Vladimir asked Ronny.

"I'm straight, " he answered. "I'll be even better once this cock sucker gets his just due."

"Don't worry, he's definitely going to be getting his issue." He stuck a cigar between his thin pink lips and put fire to the end of it. "Oh, yes, Ol' Malvo is going to get what he has coming to him." He took the cigar out of his mouth and looked at it. He loved the taste of it.

At that moment James Brown's *The Big Payback* came pumping through the speakers of the luxury vehicle.

"Turn that shit up," Ronny told the chauffer, nodding his head. He thought of how sweet his revenge on Malvo was going to be.

The volume rose and the car whisked the men.

*****

Malvo sat in the backseat of the Benz wedged between Nicolay and Mikhail. He listened to the henchmen talk about the ways they were going to torture that ass as if he wasn't sitting right there between them. Looking to his arm and leg, he saw the rags they were wrapped in were almost completely crimson. He laid his head back against the headrest and stared up at the ceiling, exhaling. His vision became blurry and his eyelids began to feel heavy. Once his eyelids had finally shut, he was able to watch the mental movie that was playing behind them. A smile curled his lips as he watched Heaven try to grab the bubbles that Faith and he blew at her. He chuckled a little seeing the look on his baby girl's face as she danced around, trying her best to capture one of the bubbles.

"Look at—look at our, baby girl," he said aloud. He continued to listen to Nicolay and Mikhail's plans to torture him as he watched the movie. When *The End* came up on the screen, darkness registered, and he lay still with a smirk etched on his face.

Tranay Adams

CHAPTER SIXTEEN

Fear held the steering wheel with one hand and used the other to fire up the blunt that dangled from his lips. He blew smoke from his nose and mouth before tossing the lighter into the ashtray. He switched hands with the L and pulled the duffle bag over into his lap from the front passenger seat. He unzipped the bag and peeked inside at all of the money wrapped in blue rubber bands.

"Fugazi," he shook his head. "Fucking fugazi."

The money Malvo had given him wasn't real and he'd always known it. The big man was fairly known in the streets. His reputation for murder and fuckery had traveled with the speed of a bullet. He remembered his face from that night outside of 7-11. He knew he was Eureka's enemy and he had planned on getting rid of him anyway. So it was a *win win* situation when word hit the concrete jungle that the head of the Greek mafia had put a bounty out on him for one hundred grand. Fear ceased the opportunity. He knew how to get in touch with Malvo because he had contacted him through a mutual acquaintance to kidnap Eureka. All he had to do was deliver him to the Greeks and collect   his   ransom.

Fear let down the window and a cool breeze rushed inside, blowing embers from his blunt. He reached inside of the duffle bag, pulling out stack after stack and throwing them into the street. He laughed looking at all of the chaos he was causing in the ghetto. People were running out into the middle of the street and into intersections trying to get to the *Root of all Evil*, narrowly missing getting hit by oncoming cars. Fear continued to throw the money until the duffle bag was empty. Afterwards, he tossed the duffle bag out into the street. He glanced up at the rearview mirror and saw people run out into the street to get their hands on the counterfeit money.

"Evil, Terror, y'all alright back there?" He looked through the rearview mirror and found the Rottweilers lying beside one another, looking around.

He cracked a grin and picked up the briefcase from off of the floor, siting it in the front passenger seat. He popped its locks and opened it. There were rows and rows of crisp hundred dollar bills inside. He grabbed one of the stacks and ran a finger across the top of it. The smell of fresh mullah brought a smile to his face. He tossed the stack back inside of the briefcase, slammed it shut and locked it. He sat the briefcase back on the floor and pulled a picture from out of his trench coat pocket. He looked back and forth from the picture of him, Eureka and Anton to the windshield.

"Man, in another life, things would have been different." He shook his head and kissed the picture, tucking it back inside of his coat. He then made a left into the parking lot of the South Bay Gallery shopping mall. He parked a couple of rows back from the side entrance and looked up through the windshield. Seeing exactly who it was he was looking for, he pulled a stocking over his face and recovered his silenced .9mm from underneath the seat. He threw open the door and hopped out. He hunched over with that thang in his hand, making hurried steps toward a couple that had emerged through the double doors of JC Penny's. The couple held hands and kissed as they headed toward the parking lot toting a shopping bag each.

"Loyalty Over Everything!"

Lavonte and Johnne's eyes bulged and their jaws dropped. Before they could scream soft whispers silenced them forever.

Choot! Choot!

Headshots dropped the couple. Fear descended upon them, popping two into each of their sternums before jogging away from the scene. Lavonte and his girl lay on the ground still holding one another's hands. Their eyes were bugged and their mouths were hanging open. They wore bleeding black holes in their foreheads and chests as if it were the latest fashion. Hot slugs were their rewards for being disloyal to Arkane.

*****

Once Eureka left the warehouse, she placed a call to Anton. She gave him specific instructions and hung up the phone. She hopped on the Metro bus which let her off two blocks down from Fear's house. She ran and walked the rest of the way. Coming upon the house, she jogged up the stairs and knocked on the door. As soon as Anton opened the door, she hugged him tightly. He looked to be taken off guard by her sudden embrace.

"Where is he?" Anton asked, holding the letter the killer had given to him.

Eureka shook her head. "I don't know. He just up and vanished."

He passed her the letter and she looked it over. It told her what she already knew, Fear was her father's murderer.

"I know."

"I can't believe this." He shook his head, wishing what he had learned wasn't real, "This whole fucking time!" He punched the doorway. Eureka stepped into the house and closed the door behind her.

"Reka is that you?" Giselle called out.

"Yeah, ma, it's me. I'll be in there in a minute." She hollered back before turning to her baby brother. "Look, we'll discuss this later, okay. Right now, I want chu to go in there with mommy."

"That's another thing. What did you want to talk to her about? You were sounding like it was some pretty heavy shit." She motioned for him to lean closer and he did. She told him exactly what Fear had told her. His eyes snapped open and his mouth formed an O as he staggered back from the devastating news. He bumped into the wall and looked up to the ceiling with teary eyes. He swallowed and closed his eyes, causing streams to shoot down his cheeks.

"I'm sorry, baby boy." Eureka embraced him, sweeping her hand up and down his back to comfort his heartache. He broke their embraced and wiped his face with his hand. "You good?" He nodded *yes.* "Alright, go in there with mommy. I'll be right back. I gotta get something."

While Anton went to tend to their mother, Eureka hurried up the staircase and dipped off into Fear's bedroom. She retrieved something from under the mattress and recovered something from out of his top dresser drawer. A moment later she rounded the doorway into the kitchen gripping a Glock. She found Anton sitting on the counter and her mother sitting at the table dipping a small white bag into a cup of tea. Giselle sat the tea bag aside. She stopped the cup at her lips as she was about to take a sip when she saw her daughter with the gun in her hand. Her eyes immediately shot up to the expression on her face. She was glassy eyed and tight lipped.

"Reka, what's going on, baby?" she asked concerned.

"You know exactly what's wrong, ma." She tossed the worn black leather case upon the table and a packet of dope. Eureka sat down at the table and slid the packet of dope toward her mother with her gun. "Go ahead. That's for   you."

Giselle looked to her son and he looked away. He was so disgusted with her he couldn't even look her in the eyes.

Giselle looked to the packet of dope, then to her daughter and her conscience told her something was wrong.

She came to her with hurtful eyes, a gun and a packet of dope. She couldn't help wondering if her baby girl had found out about her little secret and was going to make her pay for her sins.

"I guess you're wondering if that dope is laced, huh?" Eureka read her mind. "Well, wonder no more ma, I is indeed poisoned."

"Why would you do such a thing?"

"I should be asking you that."

Giselle realized that she'd discovered her shady dealings then. She knew that this day would come. She just didn't know it would come this soon.

She opened the worn leather bag and removed all of the utensils she'd need to cook up the drug. Her children watched her closely as she drew up a shot, squirting just a little   out   of   the   syringe.

"I wanna know how it went down," Eureka said.

"How what went down?" Her mother asked.

"How you paid Fear to murder daddy."

*****

Giselle entered the park with her hands in the pockets of her jeans, looking about. Once she didn't spot who she was looking for, she pulled her cell phone from her back pocket and sat down on the bench. She dialed the number of the cat that she was supposed to meet that night and discovered the line had been disconnected.

Fuck, this nigga ain't here yet? she thought. She dialed the number again and got the same result. She tucked the cell into her pocket and surveyed her surroundings. The night was cold and still. There wasn't a soul inside of the park besides her. She didn't know why but she got this eerily feeling like she wasn't alone and someone was watching her.

"This mothafucka is probably a cop and done set my ass up. I'm getting the hell up outta here."

Flap! Flap! Flap!

A pigeon came flying by her head making noises and leaving feathers floating in the air. Giselle jumped up from where she was with her heart threatening to explode. She was just about to take off when she took note that it was a pigeon. A smile graced her face as she held her hand to her chest, feeling silly. She sat back down on the bench and leaned her head back, a smile curling her lips.

"Ol' scary ass bitch." She shook her head shamefully, making fun of herself.

There was a long pause of silence and then she heard a voice.

"You're late." A distorted voice rang out. She shot to her feet again. Her head snapped back and forth, trying to locate the source of the sound.

"Who's there? Where are you?" She rattled off, eyes alive and ears alert.

"We've spoken. Now have a seat."

226

Realizing it was the cat she had come to see, Giselle did her best to calm herself and sat back down on the bench. She took a couple deep breaths and tried to relax.

"Jesus, you scared the shit outta me."

The voice's cell phone rang and he answered. "Yeah. Alright. Good."

"Is everything okay?" Giselle asked nervously.

"My partner confirmed the drop. We're good to go. Once I fulfill my end of the deal, you'll give me the other half or I'll give you an obituary. Do you understand?"

Giselle robbed, cheated, stole, sold her body and got a loan from every friend and relative she could think of to put together the twenty-five grand she'd need to pay off the hit man to carry out her husband's murder. It took her ten months but she'd finally gotten what she needed together. The way she saw things it was an investment that would net her more than enough capital to fund the lifestyle she was used to living.

"Yes." She nodded, rising to her feet with her hands in her pockets. She tried to make out the man in the darkness but she couldn't. He was draped in all black and hidden beneath the shade of a tree. All she could see was his floor length trench coat and Timberland boots. "How long before it's done?"

"A couple of days. I'll notify you once everything has been taken care of."

"Alright."

Coo! Coo! Coo!

Giselle looked to her rear and saw a quartet of pigeons. When she turned back around the man in the trench coat had vanished. Holding a hand above her brows, she peered all around and then up into the air. He'd vanished without a trace.

Coo! Coo! Coo!
The pigeons moved about making noises.

*****

"Why?" Eureka asked, wiping her wet face with the back of her hand as she held the Glock on her mother.

Giselle wiped away the tears that spilled from her eyes with her fingers and thumb. She looked up at her daughter with pink, glassy eyes. She sniffled, "What's that, baby?"

"Why did you?" Her voice cracked. The pain in her heart clogged the words in her throat stopping them from being said. A fresh set of tears ripped down her face and she wiped them away, just as fast as they appeared. She took a deep breath and gathered her wits. She closed her eyes and peeled them back open, feeling renewed. "Why did you have daddy killed?"

Giselle locked gazes with her daughter and she drew in her thoughts. She knew her thoughts like she was a psychic or something. Giselle hung her head. Her teardrops trickled hastily and splashed upon the table top. Her daughter lay back in her chair with her eyes wide and her mouth open, she was stunned. She looked away with tears dancing in her eyes. She wiped them away before looking to her mother again.

"Money." Giselle uttered.

"Really, ma? Over money?" She couldn't believe it. "How much, huh? How much was my father's life worth to you?"

Giselle looked back up at her daughter, sniffling and wiping her face with her sleeve.

"A million dollars."

"A million dollars, huh?" She sighed and shook her head. "My daddy was worth more than all of the money in the world."

"I know, baby. I know." Giselle shook as she sobbed and whimpered. "I'm sorry; I'm so sorry, baby."

"What happened to the money?"

She shook her head regretfully. "I didn't see a dime of it."

"What?" Eureka sat up in her chair.

"The policy had lapsed," Giselle confessed. Her voice cracking with emotion. She'd done a horrible thing that she couldn't take back. If she could, she'd gladly cash in her life so that her late husband could have his. As bad as she wanted it to go that way she knew that it was impossible. He was gone and he wasn't ever coming back.

"Oh, my God." Eureka cupped her hands to her face, as tears poured down her cheeks.

"My guess is your father couldn't afford to pay for it."

"Oh, noooo!" She shook her head sadly.

"I'm sorry, baby girl, if I could take it all back I would. I swear to Christ I would."

"Right. It's too late now, though." Her eyebrows arched and her nose scrunched. She looked like she'd been driven mad with cheeks slicked wet by tears. She wagged the Glock, signaling for her mother to finish with the shot. She didn't feel any sympathy for her mother. She'd been getting a pass for far too many years with her being an addict, widow and single mother, but not anymore. She had made her bed so she had to lay in it.

Giselle swallowed hard and smacked her arm until a thick vein formed. She then picked up the syringe of poison. She looked up into her daughter's face and met a pair of unforgiving eyes and twisted lips. She was looking for mercy but she sure as hell wasn't going to get it from her. Giselle looked back down at the vein in her arm as she pierced it with the needle. Blood rushed inside of the syringe and tainted the liquid the color of malt liquor. Suddenly, her head bobbed as she broke down crying, tears splashing on her tracked up arm.

"Baby girl, I swear to God."

"I don't wanna hear that shit, do it!" Eureka roared, tears cascading and rolling under her chin. She stood up and pointed the burner at her mother's face. Tightening her jaws, she spoke through clenched teeth, "Do it goddamn it, or I swear on his grave I'll open your fucking forehead up, right this minute!"

Giselle looked to Anton and he turned his head. There wouldn't be any sympathy from him either.

Sniff! Sniff! Sniff!

"Okayyy." Giselle whined, wiping her eyes and dripping nose with the back of her hand. She licked her chapped lips and mustered up the courage to do the deed. Finally, she pushed the liquid into her bloodstream. A moment later, her body went through a tantrum that threw her back in her chair. Her arms and legs thrashed around and her head shook violently. Thick foam oozed out of her mouth while blood ran out of her eyes and ears. Giselle's was jerking so hard and fast that she fell out of the chair and landed on the floor.

Thud!

Eureka lowered her banger at her side as she watched her mother's dying form take its last twitches. All she could do was stand over her as the tears slowly rolled down her face and dripped onto the floor, hitting the tip of her Timberlands. Once Giselle went still, she turned around to Anton and spread her arms.

"Ant…"

He rushed over to her and wrapped his arms around her tightly. She cried her heart out, tears dripping and staining the shoulder of his shirt. He rubbed her back and encouraged her to let it all go.

"That's it, sis, release it all. Let that shit go." He consoled her as tears danced in his own eyes.

"Ooooooh, Goddddd." Her sobs became muffled by her face being pressed into his shoulder. "Ahhhhh."

He could feel her tears seep through the fabric of his shirt. He didn't complain. He tightened his embrace and continued his gentle stroking of her back. He knew she needed to unleash all of her pinned up hurt and anger. And he didn't mind being her vessel because he loved her more than he loved the air he breathed.

Anton's eyes traveled from The Face of Death that his mother wore down to the boots on her feet. His forehead deepened with lines as he came to the realization that *the devil wore Timbs.*

Tranay Adams

CHAPTER SEVENTEEN
One month later…

Malvo's eyes peeled open and blinked under the bright lights in the ceiling. The first thing he heard was the heart monitor's beeps and several other machines at work. Feeling something over his nose and mouth, he pulled it off and discovered it was an oxygen mask. That's when he looked to his arm and found an IV. He felt where his ear once was and discovered that it had been patched and taped down. Malvo looked down and noticed he was draped in a hospital gown. He lifted the gown up and saw that he was nude underneath. His quick scan of the surroundings brought him to the conclusion he was inside of someone's bedroom. All of the windows wore gates and the floor was stripped down to the hardwood. He was in a twin size bed with one nightstand and a twenty inch flat screen that was mounted upon the wall.

Groggily, Malvo sat up in bed and checked his body for the gunshot wounds he'd passed out from due to a loss of blood. Miraculously, they all had healed. This brought a frown to his face. Because that meant he had to have been lying where he was for at least a month. But why in the hell would Vladimir want to keep him alive?

As soon as that thought went through his mind, he heard keys jingling and the door being unlocked. He yanked the IV out of his arm and attempted to remove the catheter from his dick when the door came swinging open. In came Nicolay and Mikhail. The expression on their faces told him they meant business. Malvo didn't waste any time taking a swing at one of them. Being he was still groggily, the swing was uncoordinated and sluggish. Mikhail side stepped it. He then moved in, cracking him in the jaw and nearly knocking him unconscious. He slipped under his arms and put him in the Full Nelson, locking his arms behind his head. He gave Nicolay a nod and he gave Malvo two solid blows to the gut, rocking that ass to sleep with a right to the chin. The dope peddler slipped out of the Russian's arms and onto the floor snoring fast asleep. After taking the catheter from out of his penis, they hoisted Malvo up and carried him out of the bedroom.

An hour later…

When Malvo finally came to, he looked about and found he was down in a decrepit basement. He felt the noose around his neck and the duct tape that had his wrists bound behind his back. He looked to his wobbly legs and his feet as they were trying to keep their balance on an old wooden rickety chair. He instantly felt his bladder fill with piss. He looked up to find Siska, Vladimir and their henchmen.

"Oh, shit!" Malvo said, seeing his most formidable foes. His eyes were as wide as tennis balls and he swallowed the lump in his throat. He was in for it. He didn't have to say a word because he already knew what time it was, especially once he saw Ronny descending the staircase slowly. He came to stand between Vladimir and Siska. The Russian drug lord handed him a pistol. *Click! Clack!* He chambered a round into the head of the weapon. Once he did this, Siska and Vladimir brandished guns of their own and cocked the slides on them.

Blam! Blam! Boc! Boc! Pop! Pop!

The basement wafted with gun smoke as the weapons grew still. All could be heard was the squealing of the rickety chair as it was on its last leg. There was only one wooden rod keeping it from collapsing. Malvo looked down at his feet. The way the seat was moving it was like he was riding it on the waves of the ocean. Bug eyed, he swallowed hard and looked at Ronny.

Malvo shut his eyes and recited a prayer.

"Cock suckers turn religious when they're confronted with death." Vladimir laughed hardily and nudged Siska. Siska looked to him and started laughing, nudging him back. Even Ronny had caught the funny bug. The henchmen were doubled over laughing as well.

The staircase squeaked as someone slowly descended it. Then suddenly a pair of feet came hurrying down the steps causing Vladimir, Siska and their henchmen's heads to whip around. Their eyes grew big and their mouths expanded in shock. Their bodies turned as they went to fire on the advancing threat.

Choot! Choot! Choot! Choot! Choot! Choot! Choot! Choot!

"Gaaaa!"

"Argggh!"

"Ahhhh!"

Vladimir and Siska went down fast and bloody as a hooded man let his silenced machine gun go ham. Hot bullets ripped through tissue and red sprays misted the air. Ronny spun on the henchman nearest to him, smacking the burner out of his hand. He wrapped his arm around his neck and raised his banger letting that heat go crazy. *Boc! Boc! Boc! Boc!* They went down in a blink of an eye but not before they pumped the henchman he was using as a human shield full of holes. Ronny kicked the human shield in his ass, sending him crashing into the last henchman. The human shield collided into the last henchman as he was busting at Ronny. The wounded man and the henchman went falling back with him blazing his tool in the air.

"You good?" Ronny asked of his secret accomplice. They nodded *yes*.

He then looked to the man that was lying beneath the riddled human shield. Grimacing with bloody lips, the man struggled to get from beneath the dead body but to no avail. Suddenly, he stopped and looked up as a shadow eclipsed him. His eyes bulged and his mouth widen. He gasped as Ronny aimed that thang at his dome piece and smiled   wickedly.

Boc! Boc! Boc!

Malvo cringed and turned his head, seeing the man's head burst like a rotten tomato. When his eyes popped back open, they saw a wincing Vladimir about to shoot Ronny in the back.

The hooded villain cut loose with something loud and dangerous causing the blonde haired man to fall back and drop his gun. It slid across the floor spinning around in circles. Ronny snapped around with a scowling face and twisted lips. He looked to the sprawled Russian drug lord and then to his comrade's smoking machine gun. He gave a nod before proceeding toward Vladimir who was staring up at him gasping for air.

Ronny pointed his ratchet right at the Russian's forehead.

"Now, I know you didn't think I was gon' let that sit slide, did ya?"

A quick flashback of what Vladimir's henchmen had done to him back at the chop shop and the basement went through his mental.

Boc! Boc! Boc! Boc!

236

Ronny took the time to admire his handiwork before letting the banger drop to the floor. He then turned around to his former boss fishing around inside of his pocket until he withdrew a straight razor, opening it. Its blade gleamed beneath the soft light of the basement.

"It's yo turn, Big Poppa," he said, stepping around the last of his victims. Malvo's head snapped all around trying to figure out where his street son had disappeared to. Suddenly, his eyes went wide like they were trying to jump out of his head.

"Ahhh! Ahhh!" Malvo's head jumped higher and higher with each swipe of the straight razor that severed his Achilles tendons, causing his knees to bend. Tears in his eyes, he looked down and saw his feet in blood. He heard a crate being dragged over and then being stepped upon. He tried to turn to Ronny but he was on his blindside. Feeling a firm hold on the noose around his neck, he looked up and saw his hand around it as he was cutting it with the razor. Suddenly, the rope came loose. Malvo tried to keep standing but ended up falling face first, busting his grill. He grimaced when he brought his face back up from the surface, spitting loose red teeth. His tongue felt around in his bleeding mouth feeling all of the missing teeth. His eyes paid close attention to Ronny as he stepped over him, closing the straight razor and approaching the hooded stranger.

"You alright?" The hooded person asked him. Ronny nodded *yes*.

Malvo frowned seeing Ronny pull the person close and kiss them in the mouth. "You ready?" Ronny asked.

"Yep." A feminine voice responded before slinging the strap of the machine gun over her shoulder. Shee then reached beneath her hoodie and withdrew a thick stick. She made her way toward Malvo pulling the hood from her head and revealing her identity. When the dope dealer saw her face, he couldn't believe it. His jaw dropped and he blinked over and over again. He then felt shit threatening to come bursting through his asshole. He was so choked up he could barely form the words he wanted to say.

"Y—you," he managed to stammer out.

"That's right, me." She smiled mischievously as she tapped the stick into her palm. "Antoinette you scumbag rapist."

Malvo felt movement at his back and his eyes darted to their corners. The next thing he knew there was something heavy being placed between his shoulders. Ronny had sat a hundred pound weight there. He then pulled up his hospital gown exposing his big hairy ass cheeks.

Smack!

"All of that ass, my nigga, you should have been sliding down the poles at Starz." He declared with a smile after smacking his buttocks. He then posted up by the staircase and sparked up a blunt as he watched the show. Antoinette got down on her knees behind Malvo and slid his legs apart with her knee. He tried to escape but with his tendons severed and the weight on his back that was impossible.

"Wa—wait—" Malvo shouted out as he twisted his head around as far as he could. His eyes were consumed by terror and he was clenching his cheeks as tightly as he could.

"Nah, I don't have a condom, and you not gone be straight after this either." Madness danced in her glassy eyes as she bit down into her bottom lip. "Just let me get this thang off." She repeated the exact same words to him he'd used when he'd raped her.

"No, please, I—"

With a grunt, Antoinette shoved the stick into his rectum, violently. His eyes grew so wide his pupils looked smaller than they were. His mouth fell open and he lips quivered. "Ggggaaa! Arghh." He squirmed in agony as she worked the stick back and forth inside of him, fucking him unmercifully with it.

"Shut up! I don't wanna hear no more back talk!" She told him like he'd told her.

"Ahhhhh." His eyes welled up with tears and spilled down his cheeks. He clenched his teeth and his buttocks even tighter but it was useless, she was all up in him, punishing his sacred place.

"Uh! Uh! Uh!" Creases ran through her forehead and wrinkles formed around her nose. Her face shined as she was building up a sweat, jamming the stick further into his anus. The friction stretched the skin around the once tightened hole and blood ran with a vengeance. Feces and blood clung to the stick. Malvo pissed on himself and a combination of overwhelming smells invaded the room.

Antoinette would have gagged had it not been for her being lost in the throngs of revenge. "You ready for this cum, bitch, huh?" Again she mocked him with tears streaming down her face relentlessly, working that stick like a plunger inside of a toilet, mangling his asshole. "Uh! Uh! Uh!" Further and further and further, the stick went inside of his stinker. "I can't hear you, sweetheart! You gotta speak up if you wanna be heard!"

"Gaa—uh—arrgh!" The air from his flaring nostrils and his hot breath blew the debris below him. He was as helpless as a newborn baby. All he could do was lie there as she brutalized his brown eye.

"Here, I come, Big Daddy. Here.I. Fucking. Cum!"

Snappp!

The stick broke in half and she fell on her back, still holding on to the other half. She scrambled to her feet just as Ronny started in her direction. En route to Antoinette, he spared Malvo a glance and found half of the stick lodged up his ass.

"You fucking asshole! I hate chu!" She threw the stick at Malvo's back and kicked him hard in his ribs, drawing a howl of pain from him. She then broke down sobbing, tears dripping and shoulders rocking. Ronny embraced her with one arm, hugging her into him tightly. She wailed loud and hard, but her voice was muffled by the fabric of his shirt. She then pulled away, wiping her face with the back of her hand.

"You alright, baby?" He looked into her eyes as he caressed the side of her face. She walked over to the dope peddler and kicked him hard in his ribs again. She'd broken a couple of them this time as she could hear them breaking. For good measure, she harped up phlegm and spat on him.

"Much better now."

"I got this. You go keep the car running." He kissed her on the lips and forehead, sending her on her way.

Antoinette stopped as she reached the staircase and turned to her boo. "I love you."

"I love you too, baby," he replied.

"Not as much as I love you."

"Impossible."

She smiled and he smiled back. With that she was gone.

Ronny grabbed a red gas can from the corner of the

basement and began splashing the floors, the dead bodies and the walls with gasoline. He then slowly backed up the staircase dousing them with the flammable fluid. Once he finished, he tossed the gas can aside. He pulled out a match-book and struck a match. He took the time to admire the burning flame before turned his hateful eyes onto his former boss, smiling devilishly. The flickering golden glow of the flame inside of the dimly lit space made him look like the devil. His eyes went from the flame to Malvo, lying on the basement floor. He looked as helpless as a fly with its wings torn off.

"Ron—Ronny," Malvo croaked with his last attempt to plead his case.

"See ya, wouldn't wanna be ya." Ronny tossed the match. It hit the clear liquid and *Froooosh*.

Malvo watched the fire cook the water heater causing its plastic to bubble. Abruptly, it exploded. The house went up and with it went Malvo and his reign of terror.

Tranay Adams

EPILOGUE
Four years later...

His fists looked like blurs as he worked the speed bag, eyes focused, forehead beaded with sweat. Although he was beating on the bag, he envisioned himself breaking his father's killer off something real proper like. The funny thing was his opponent was the hardest one he'd faced yet and their scrapping was one of the toughest brawls he'd ever experienced in his life.

He knew the day would come that they would lock ass and he wanted to be especially prepared for that date.

After Fear's disappearance, Anton picked up exactly where he'd left off. He got contracts from the likes of some of the most powerful and influential men around the world. They paid handsomely which allowed him to take good care of his family and move into the enormous mansion he was in. With all of the money he'd made, he could have easily fell back from the murder game but it was something about the thrill of the hunt that kept his heart beating. He didn't see himself turning his back on the game anytime soon. Far as he was concerned, he was going to ride it out until he saw a 6 x 9 or a grave.

Bunk! Bunk! Bunk! Bunk! Bunk!

Anton jabbed the speed bag one last time before drying off with the white towel and unwrapping his fists. He was now twenty years old and had changed considerably since he was fifteen. He stood five foot ten and sported an athletic physique. Over the years he'd grown in knowledge, wisdom and strength.

Buzzzzzzz!

He hung his towel around his neck and approached

the intercom. He held down the button. "What's up, sis?"

"Dinners ready, baby boy." Eureka responded.

He held the button down. "Alright, I'ma shower and head on up."

"See ya then."

After hitting the shower which was located at the back of the gym, Anton got dressed in a throwback Chicago Bulls jersey Michael Jordan 23, gray sweat and a pair of 13s. He took the elevator upstairs and walked across the enormous living room en route to the kitchen. On his way there, he could smell the delicious meal his sister prepared. As soon as he crossed the threshold into the kitchen, he was greeted by their little addition.

"Uncle Ant, where you been?" The brown skinned three year old sitting at the table asked. Eureka had just sat a plate of lasagna, garlic bread and Caesar salad before him. "I've been looking all over for you?"

Anton cracked a smile. "I was down in the gym, chump, waiting on you. You must of gotten scared I was gon' whip your butt." He threw phantom punches at the kid and he hopped up out of his chair, swinging back. He laughed and giggled as he tried his best to put hands on his uncle. The little guy was quite nice with his hands. This was because Anton would get up every morning and train him down in the gym. He was teaching him other things as well, but they kept that between them because if the boy's mother was to ever find out she'd wring her baby brother's neck.

Anton amused his nephew bobbing and weaving his punches, all the while watching his foot work. He was pleased to see he had picked up the skills he'd taught and he was confident one day he'd find out if he remembered his other lessons as well.

Eureka smiled looking at the most important men in her life playing around. She sat Anton's plate and his glass of juice down on the table and folded her arms across her chest, watching them.

Little man swung and Anton faked like he had connected with his chin, falling out on the floor. Seeing this, his nephew shadowboxed and showed off his footwork, as if he'd really put in some work on his opponent.

"Reka," Anton whispered with one eye open, getting his sister's attention.

"Yeah?" she whispered back.

"Start the count."

"Oh, sure thing."

Anton closed both of his eyes pretending to be knocked out. She stood over him counting while her offspring continued with his shadow boxing. Once she was done, she held up her son's arm. "And the winner by knockout ladies and gentlemen, Kingston 'Steel Hands' Jackson."

Kingston stood there smiling as his mother and uncle made sounds of a crowd roaring in excitement.

40 minutes later...

The Jacksons had eaten and chatted after. Everyone was good and full.

Kingston and Eureka were laughing at Anton's telling of a funny story when the little boy noticed his uncle's hand. The sight of it made his forehead wrinkle a bit.

"Uncle Ant."

Anton came down from his laughter. "What's up, my man?"

"How'd you get those scars?" he asked curiously.

Anton looked at his hand. It bared missing knuckles, scars, and burn marks. He made his hand into a fist and sat it down on the desk top.

"Surviving. I fight to survive."

"Why do you survive?"

"So I can live and be able to take care of my family."

"Whose fam?"

"You and your mother." His motioned a finger between them.

"Oh," he said, picking up his glass of juice and taking a drink.

Eureka and Anton exchanged glances smiling.

She looked at her watch and frowned." It's getting late. I needed to get him in the tub."

"Alright, I'll take care of the dishes." Anton rose to his feet.

"Thanks." Eureka told him, taking Kingston's hand. "Come on, baby, let's get chu washed up and in bed."

She disappeared through the kitchen's door and he went on to wash the dishes. Once he was done, he dried his hands off, killed the light and headed out of the door.

*****

The elevator stopped in a dimly lit underground bunker and the doors separated. There was a black on black H2 Hummer, a Cadillac Escalade truck, and a motorcycle. All of these vehicles were polished to a fine black and sitting on some pretty chrome thangs. The illumination from the lights in the ceiling caused the chrome and the paint on them to gleam. Anton cracked a grin as he walked past the motorcycle dragging his hand across its shiny handle bars. Out of all of his toys, the bike was his favorite and he drove it the most. Anton approached a control board that was lit up like the control panel on the space ship on Star Trek. Over it there was a screen showing all angles of his mansion in squares. He had the best in surveillance cameras and home security systems. If a nigga was caught sneaking on his premises, then that was his ass. Anton looked over the screen to make sure his estate was good. He then looked down a row of neon lit switches, flipping them on one by one.

Flipping on the switch shined light on something behind a display glass that stretched across the entire wall. Anton approached the display, looking through the glass as he walked the length of it. He walked past a bow gun, a katana, a shield, a shotgun, and a suit of body armor and a black mask with goggles and a breathing mask. A utility belt was around it waist. Attached to it on one side was a nightstick and on the other was a holstered automatic handgun. He stopped and admired the suit of armor. It was one of many he wore when duty called. Anton's hand caressed the glass as he admired the suit before he moved on. His eyes came across the book that Fear had them read to gain the knowledge of century's worth of assassins. Next there was a wrinkled letter. This was the letter that was inside of the envelope the hit man had stuck inside of his pocket when he slipped him something that knocked him out cold.

Anton read the letter for what seemed like the millionth time.

Little Brother if only you knew how hard it was for me to tell you this. Words cannot begin to explain the sorrow feel or the way my heart bleeds just thinking of what I am about to reveal. Although it pains me, it is only right that I tell you the truth. I am the one that killed your father.

The letter then went on to explain his mother's involvement and how terribly sorry he was and how he wished he could take what had happened back.

Knowing you, I know you're in your feelings right now. And I can't say that I blame you, you've got every right to be. You can hate me as much as you want because I deserve it. And should the day come where hating me just isn't enough for you anymore then me and you can settle this man to man, killer to killer, student to teacher.

Fearless

Anton's face contorted to something demonic as he gritted his teeth and balled his fingers into a fist. Veins spread up his neck and forehead as his head slightly shook. With a growl, he punched the glass with his fist causing it to crack like a spider's web. Blood seeped from his slice knuckles and ran into the crevasses of the broken glass.

"I'm coming for you," he said, nostrils widening and decreasing as his jaws swelled. He looked up to the ceiling, clenching his fists tightly and screaming.

"I'm commminggg for youuuuuuu!" His voice echoed and bounced off of the walls inside of the bunker.

*****

Rio de Janeiro, Brazil...

Fear's eyes snapped open and he stared up at the ceiling for a while. He'd grown a thick crop of hair which he wore in a bun and a beard so full and long it tickled his chest. He was as naked as the day he was snatched out of his mother's womb. Lying in bed on both sides of him was last night's entertainment, two of the most beautiful Brazilian whores he'd ever have the privilege of laying eyes on. Fear slid out of bed and poured himself a glass of Tequila. He took the bottle to the head, drinking the last of the alcohol it had left and swallowing the worm that was held prisoner inside. He took a sip from his glass and headed over to the small table and chair in the corner, cock swing from left to right. He moved around the room like a nigga that was fully clothed. He reached inside of the breast pocket of his plaid shirt that was hanging onto the back of the chair. When his hand came back up it was holding a picture of him and Anton. They were standing back to back holding guns and making tough faces.

He took a sip of his drink as he stared down at the picture. "I'll be waiting."

To Be Continued...
The Devil Wears Timbs 4
The Realest Killaz

Tranay Adams

AVAILABLE NOW BY TRANAY ADAMS

The Devil Wears Timbs 1-5

Bury Me A G 1-3

Tyson's Treasure 1-2

Treasure's Pain

A South Central Love Affair

Me And My Hittas 1- 6

The Last Real Nigga Alive 1-3

Fangeance

Fearless

COMING SOON BY TRANAY ADAMS

The Devil Wears Timbs 6: Just Like Daddy

A Hood Nigga's Blues

Bloody Knuckles

Billy Bad Ass

Tranay Adams

Made in the USA
Middletown, DE
28 July 2021